"Well, there is not much that compares to the freedom you feel riding full out on your own mount across an open field with the sun beaming on your face and the wind whipping through your hair. I hope I get to see that moment. That will be a sight to behold."

Catriona sucked in an unsteady breath. The way Ewan looked at her, as if he knew things about her that she did not even know about herself, sent every fiber of her being aflame.

"And you, my laird, what is it that would set your spirit free?" She walked alongside him, her fingertips accidentally skimming the back of his hand for the briefest of touches.

He paused.

"Honestly?" he asked, stepping closer.

"Aye," she whispered.

"Kissing you."

Her breath hitched in her throat, and she swallowed hard. "Then why don't you?"

He stared devilishly at her lips as if they were water itself before meeting her gaze. "I know I couldn't stop myself at just one kiss."

His gaze held images of such abandon, and she released a breath. "Then I am grateful for your restraint," she answered, leaning forward until her breath blew across his cheek. "Let us see how long it holds for both of us."

Author Note

Conveniently Wed to the Laird begins in the bustling streets of Edinburgh, Scotland, six months after the end of *The Lost Laird from Her Past*. Ewan Stewart is the new laird of his clan after the passing of his father and struggling under the yoke of such responsibility. He knows he needs to find a bride, settle into his new role and take command of his people before it is yanked away from him, but he hesitates at every turn.

Catriona Gordon is an orphan unused to kindness or trust, but is fiercely self-reliant. She longs for safety, but most of all, freedom. Despite having been married, she has never loved a man and doesn't even really believe in the idea of it. When she and Ewan are thrust into each other's lives, everything they believed about their future and their own possible happiness is turned on its head.

This book ended up being a story about the awkward and sometimes painful beauty of family, whether it be by birth or by choice, or any of the variations in between, and how all of them should be cherished and celebrated, no matter how imperfect they may be.

JEANINE ENGLERT

—

Conveniently Wed to the Laird

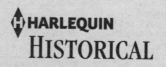

Recycling programs
for this product may
not exist in your area.

ISBN-13: 978-1-335-72370-3

Conveniently Wed to the Laird

Copyright © 2023 by Jeanine Englert

For questions and comments about the quality of this book,
please contact us at CustomerService@Harlequin.com.

Harlequin Enterprises ULC
22 Adelaide St. West, 41st Floor
Toronto, Ontario M5H 4E3, Canada
www.Harlequin.com

Printed in U.S.A.

Jeanine Englert's love affair with mysteries and romance began with Nancy Drew and her grandmother's bookshelves of romance novels. When she isn't wrangling with her characters, she can be found trying to convince her husband to watch her latest Masterpiece/BBC show obsession. She loves to talk about writing, her beloved rescue pups, as well as mysteries and romance with readers. Visit her website at www.jeaninewrites.com.

Books by Jeanine Englert

Harlequin Historical

The Highlander's Secret Son

Falling for a Stewart

Eloping with the Laird
The Lost Laird from Her Past
Conveniently Wed to the Laird

Visit the Author Profile page
at Harlequin.com.

To the Englert, Ambrose, Tarlton,
West and Williams families:

Thank you for welcoming me into your homes
and hearts when I married Brian so many years
ago. Your unconditional love, encouragement and
kindness has always overwhelmed me in the best
of ways. I am so grateful to have you as family.

And to Brent:

I always wonder what conversations we might
have had and about all the things the world has
missed out on without you in it. Your time on this
earth was far too short. We miss you, always.

Chapter One

Edinburgh, Scotland, June 1744

'Is that all of it, then?' asked Ewan Stewart, Laird of Glenhaven, staring out of the carriage window and summoning the last thread of his patience. This *brief* holiday to Edinburgh to aid his sister in her wedding preparations had become anything but. He'd be lucky to be home by week's end. The sun was high in the early afternoon sky.

'I've only one last errand to the milliner's shop, brother.' Brenna patted his hand as if he were but a child and not her older brother and laird of the clan. '*You* insisted on joining me on this journey. I could have been escorted by your men instead.'

He scoffed and moved away from the window and deeper into the plush squabs. 'Aye. You could have, but after being attack by mercenaries during your unchaperoned carriage ride through Loch Linnhe last fall, your fiancé and I agreed this was necessary to ensure your safety. We cannot risk losing you again.'

'Brother, none of that was my fault or yours. No one could have foreseen such events,' she complained.

He lifted his brow at her.

'Not even you,' she said.

'I am not as certain. Father should have suspected such foul play from Mr Winters due to the man's eagerness to secure a match with you. We will be far more vigilant about who moves within our inner ranks from now on.'

Knowing whom to trust in the Highlands was not as easy as it used to be. After Brenna's brush with death at the hands of brigands trying to destroy their clan from within last winter, her fiancé Garrick and Ewan had vowed to keep close watch over her. Neither of them could bear another loss. The last year had been rife with them.

'As you wish. Perhaps you could turn your attentions to finding a bride, brother, rather than my affairs. There seem many eligible ladies about.' She smiled innocently.

Ewan frowned at her well-placed barb. He was less than eager to find a wife after almost sacrificing everything to be with a woman who cast him aside like a worn-down horseshoe when a better prospect came along. After his experience with Emogene, he no longer trusted his judgement about women or love, and his sister knew it. 'I hope all of the hats are too small for your head,' he said, mirroring the same feigned sweetness in his reply as she had in her own.

'You shall not snare a bride with a forked tongue like that.' She waited for the carriage to come to a rocking stop, her face softening in concern as she studied him.

'Do try to enjoy what remains of our visit if you can. You have been so dour as of late, and who knows when we shall return.' She pressed a light kiss to his cheek. The door opened, and their driver assisted her exit onto the bustling streets of Edinburgh.

He muttered a response and watched her enter the milliner's shop. Resting back against the seat, he sighed. At least the trip had not been an entire waste of time. He had met with a few businesses regarding investments for the clan yesterday after they had arrived. He had also called on the solicitor earlier this morn during Brenna's dress fitting to apprise himself of the pending taxes and the clan's current financial situation. While the clan was in good standing for now, changes would have to be made for it to remain that way.

Changes some would oppose. There were more than a few leaders within the clan who would be rankled by his suggestions to bring the mining and farming techniques up to modern standards. But he also knew that if things didn't change, tradition would put a stranglehold on their growth and advancement. They'd be overpowered and absorbed by other clans or worse, the British. He'd need to earn their trust. They held great power and sway over the village. Without their support, Ewan had a slim chance of making the changes that would help their clan survive. The problem was that they didn't trust him, and they had good reason not to.

Ewan had almost brought the clan to its knees years ago when he'd gone against his father's orders and courted Emogene despite the arranged marriage set up with the Robertson clan prior to Ewan's birth. By not marrying the laird's daughter, Ewan had severed the Stewarts' alliance and fractured his relationship with his father: all for love, for her. And then Emogene had tossed him aside as if he were rubbish to secret herself away and marry a Sutherland. She'd left him for a man with more power and larger purse strings.

And even though they never married, the damage had already been done, and the alliance between the Stewarts and the Robertsons fractured to bits. His face heated with the shame he still felt over what he'd done. He'd not be that foolish over a woman ever again.

Ewan scoffed and turned the gold signet ring on his third finger. He'd not survive another misstep such as that, so making decisions about the clan exhausted and oft-times overwhelmed him. So many people he loved and cared about depended on him making sound decisions. Unfortunately, finances were but one of the clan's many issues that Father should have warned him of before he died, but Ewan wasn't terribly surprised by the omissions. Father wasn't one for addressing any weaknesses, within himself or the clan, and abhorred the idea of lingering too long on any problems he couldn't immediately glean a solution to. Being laird didn't have quite the shine to it Ewan had expected, but he'd keep at it. Surely it would get easier, and finding his place in this world would as well.

He tugged at his cravat. Restless, he emerged from the carriage and stretched, scanning the busy streets. Perhaps Brenna was right about one thing: he should try to enjoy their visit. Who knew when they would have the time to travel to and from the city again? The

Grassmarket was within sight down the hill, and he watched lads handing out penny broadsides shouting bawdy headlines and men peddling their wares of live-stock, trinkets, and the occasional oddity in the warm early afternoon sun.

Ewan walked a few steps, studying the area teem-ing with life and excitement below, a far cry from the rather subdued Highland markets. He itched to explore the sights and soak up something new and interesting. But leaving Brenna was a risk. The lass attracted chaos like his other sister attracted order. And he attracted... well, he wasn't quite sure yet. The three of them were quite an odd trio, but they were family. And he was bound by duty and his promise to his father to protect them at all costs.

'You must keep the family together and this clan thriving after I am gone,' Father had pleaded before his heart gave out. *'Promise me.'*

Like a fool, Ewan had agreed and made such a prom-ise. Months later, he found the task daunting as his spirited sisters set out on their own pursuits. His sister Moira was with her husband, Laird Rory McKenna, in Oban, and soon Brenna would be wed to her fiancé, Laird Garrick MacLean, and reside in Loch Linnhe. That meant he would be all alone as Laird of Glen-haven, attempting to keep the Stewart clan and its leg-acy afloat. At almost eight and twenty, he knew he *should* take a wife, but the thought of choosing one woman to spend the rest of his days with made his chest tighten and his body shudder.

What if he chose wrong again like he had with Emogene? He was laird, and any mistakes he made in love or otherwise would cost him and his clan dearly. And with times as difficult as they were now, mistakes could end the Stewarts.

Forever.

He'd seen clans disappear from existence, as if they had walked into the Highland mist, never to return.

'I can keep watch on her, my laird.'

Ewan shook off his melancholy and glanced up to the driving box of the carriage and then back at the milliner's store. Brenna was never one to decide quickly upon anything, so he had some time. Perhaps some air and the renewed flow of blood through his limbs would restore his humour and distract him from his fears. 'Aye, thank you, Aaron. I'll just stretch my legs.'

His driver nodded to him, and Ewan rolled his neck. He tucked his hands into the pockets of his trews and settled into the feel of the cobblestones beneath his boots. The hard, firm, unrelenting pressure was a reminder that not all was lost. Not yet. The Stewarts were bedrock. As such, they would endure. As would he. The tension abated with each step as if the yoke of responsibility loosened, slipping away the farther he was from the carriage with its Stewart coat of arms. The June sun warmed his cheeks. The sights and smells of cooked meats, leather, and coal from the market swallowed him as he approached. A lad pressed a broadside into his hand, and Ewan gave him a penny.

Ewan scanned the sheet and frowned. *A wife for sale?* What a farce. One couldn't buy a wife, not in Scotland, at least. And why would one want to? He shuddered. He tucked the sheet into his coat pocket and carried on his way. He'd take another minute to look about the wares and return to the carriage.

'Wife for sale! One guinea!' a man shouted.

Ewan turned. A small crowd formed around a stout older man as he yanked a young woman behind him. She wore a leather halter like one used for livestock, and her hands were bound in front of her. Ewan froze, shocked and angered by the sight of a woman being treated thus. He fisted his hands by his sides. Surely this was some ill-humoured jest.

She was a person, not a mule. If this was what happened at the Grassmarket, he'd missed nothing.

But on it continued. 'I be 'er husband. She be foulmouthed, prone to laziness, and disobedient, despite me best efforts to make her so. I'll be pleased to be rid of 'er. Once ye purchase 'er, she is divorced from me and bound to ye by marriage. So, take heed with yer coin! Yer purchase is final. No returns for this lass.' He released a bawdy laugh.

Ewan studied the pale, thin woman clad in dirty, worn clothes, her long hair falling loose from its light auburn plait and shielding part of her face like a veil. He wondered what would become of her. A flare of protectiveness flashed through him. Surely this wasn't legal. He tugged the crumpled broadside from his pocket and scanned it. He balked.

According to this, it was. The single exchange of coin nullified the first union and verified the new marriage. He could scarcely imagine such a concept. Several men approached to gaze more closely at her, their interest evident in their stances and overt ogling. One tugged at her skirts, attempting to peek beneath, and she kicked the sot in the head. He staggered back and cursed at her.

Ewan scrubbed a hand through his hair, and his pulse picked up speed. This was someone's daughter. Someone's sister. But where were they? His gaze swept through the growing crowd that jeered and spat at her. It appeared there was no one to speak out on her behalf. She was alone. Defenceless.

Just like Moira.

He felt the familiar anguish and tightening in his chest with the memory of his eldest sister's abuse at the hands of her first husband. Ewan's awareness and rage sharpened to a fine point. If he'd known what was happening to her, he would have stopped it, but he'd not found out until it was too late. And he'd never forgive himself for that. But this? What about all these people? How could they merely watch this woman's suffering and not intervene on her behalf?

'Ye see 'er disobedience!' the husband shouted as another keen buyer came too close and the woman elbowed the man in the gut. 'I am eager to be rid of this bony, cold, ungrateful lass and find another, more willing woman to warm my bed. One guinea! Step right up and claim 'er if ye dare.'

'I'll take her for half that,' a man called off in the distance. The crowd opened for him, and when Ewan saw the man's face, he cursed.

Dallan MacGregor.

A cheat and a brute, among other things.

Ewan clenched his jaw. He'd known the bampot since

childhood, and MacGregor had only become crueller with age. Rumours still abounded around his involvement in the death of a young woman at last year's royal ball in Perth, even though he was never charged with the crime. There was a reason no father allowed his daughter to marry MacGregor, despite his coin. Perhaps that was why he was attempting to buy a wife now. Although Ewan couldn't imagine she would survive long under the bastard's care.

'Any other bidders?' the husband called to the crowd.

Silence answered.

Dallan grinned, grabbed the lass's wrist, and yanked her to him. 'Seems a bit thin to warm my bed, but I will make use of her. She will learn to obey me.'

She pushed him and tried to stomp on his foot. He grabbed her by the hair to subdue her, and she cried out in protest.

'Kneel,' he commanded, yanking on her hair again.

She whimpered and fell to her knees.

'You see, we are already coming to an understanding.' He laughed, fishing for coin in his pocket. A few other men in the crowd cheered him on.

Ewan's heart thudded in his chest, and his ears buzzed. The lass would be dead by week's end if MacGregor had his way with her, and who would know or care?

He would.

Ewan cursed aloud. He knew what he had to do. It was the lesser of two evils.

'I'll buy her for the full,' he called out, his voice booming across the market.

Dallan stilled, and upon catching Ewan's gaze through the crowd, he smirked. 'Stewart,' he said. He shoved the lass away. She stumbled and skidded to the ground from the force.

Ewan clenched his jaw. His gaze slid to the woman, who, although startled, seemed unhurt, and then back to Dallan. 'I see you haven't changed, MacGregor,' he stated, squaring his shoulders upon approach.

'Neither have you.' Dallan spat at the ground and ran a hand through his hair. 'Still as soft a heart as ever. Do you plan to save this whore as well as your dwindling clan from ruin now that your father is gone? Not likely. Enjoy your wench and your brief reign as laird. I'll save my half a guinea.' He laughed and sauntered off with two of his men in tow.

'Bring her here,' Ewan commanded, rage lacing his words. The crowd turned to him.

The lass's eyes widened as her husband yanked her up from the ground. She clambered after him, holding the rope of the harness fitted to her torso as she was tugged along.

'Unbind her hands and remove that ungodly harness from her. *Now*,' Ewan ordered. 'She is no animal.'

'Ye might think differently after ye get her home.' The man winked at him. 'I'll leave 'er be. Otherwise she'll run.'

Ewan scowled at him and shoved a guinea into the man's open palm, even though he wished to punch him in the face instead.

'Pleasure doin' business with ye.' The man grinned

and pressed the guinea to his lips. 'I shall celebrate my freedom this eve!'

Ewan shook his head in disgust as the man walked away. He faced the lass. 'Are you hurt?'

'Nay,' she answered, slowly lifting her gaze to him.

Her large amber eyes arrested his attention. He'd never seen such a shade before.

He cleared his throat. 'Come with me,' he told the woman. He turned and began the walk back to the carriage, his body vibrating with anger.

'What shall you do with me, sir?' the woman asked, walking a step behind him. He slowed his pace to ensure she didn't drift far from him, his gaze sliding behind him at regular intervals. Dallan was not a man to lose at anything well, and Ewan wouldn't allow the woman to be harmed further.

'I'm not sure yet, but you'll not stay here.' He didn't dare spare her another glance but kept a quick pace up the road to the carriage. He'd had enough of his brief visit to the Grassmarket. He'd had enough of a great deal of things.

A bell chimed ahead of them as Brenna emerged from the milliner's shop door and handed off her parcels to Aaron. When she turned and saw their approach, she froze, her mouth falling open.

'Aaron, get my sister inside,' Ewan ordered as he reached the carriage. 'I also need a larger blade than my sgian dubh. *Now.*'

'Aye, my laird.' His driver's gaze landed upon the lass for a moment before flitting away. 'Miss?' He opened the door for Brenna, who still stood gobsmacked.

'Brother, I leave you for one moment,' she muttered, shading her eyes from the sun as her dark hair fluttered in the wind. 'What has happened?'

'In the carriage, Brenna. We are leaving,' Ewan commanded.

'Brother?' she faltered, still staring upon the woman.

'The carriage,' he answered, the edge in his voice as sharp as any dirk. Her eyes widened at his harsh tone, and she clamped her mouth shut and did as he instructed.

Once she was safely within, Aaron retrieved a large dagger from beneath his driver's seat and handed it to Ewan.

'Your wrists,' he stated, his tone harsher than he intended.

The woman hesitated and then lifted them to him, keeping her head down.

He took her left hand, then paused at the sight of the numerous scars along her knuckles and calluses on her fingers. His thumb skimmed the soft inside of her wrist as he severed the rope. Her tremble at his touch passed through his arm, and he let go.

The lass had been poorly treated. For how long, he didn't know. Nor did it matter. That would end today.

'Turn,' he said, his voice softening. The last thing he wished to do was frighten her further.

She hesitated, turning slowly as if she half expected a shove or slap. He stared at the bindings of the worn leather harness criss-crossed along her back. How could a woman live such a life, and why? He shuddered to think how long she might have lived this way. He shook away the thought and brought himself back to the present.

He swallowed hard and slid his hand between the rope and her tattered walking dress, her body flinching at his touch. She possessed a small, muscular, thin frame, and he tugged the rope away from her body as gently as he could. The harness was so tight, he struggled to do so with care. *Blast.* He didn't wish to harm her.

'Go on,' she murmured. 'It doesn't hurt. Not any more.'

His touch faltered at her words, and he held back the tyranny of curses bubbling up in his throat. *What kind of a man...?* He answered his own question. He knew exactly the type. Ewan severed the taunt harness bindings. When they fell away from her body, the woman sighed, her body sagging forward. He wished to beat her former husband senseless, but he needed to get out of here. Far from here before he did just that and brought shame and ruin to his clan. He was laird. He needed to focus on his clan and his family, not this stranger who was now in his care, or her brute of a husband. He stilled.

Now *he* was her husband.

Shock roiled through him. What had he done?

What he'd had to.

To do nothing would have haunted him the rest of his days. He only hoped this decision wouldn't as well.

'Step inside, miss,' he said, gesturing at the still-open carriage door.

She nodded and stepped within, settling in neatly next to his sister.

Brenna looked at her and then to Ewan without a

word, although her wide eyes held the thousand questions he knew she wished to ask.

'Well, sister,' he offered, as Aaron set the carriage in motion towards Glasgow. 'You told me to find a bride, so I did.'

Chapter Two

'What?' the woman asked, crinkling her nose. 'One cannot find a wife in the time it takes me to purchase a hat.' She rolled her eyes at the man and straightened her light blue cloak over her gown as the carriage lurched forward. Her fine gloved hands fluttered like a dove's wings before settling in her lap.

Catriona Gordon bit her lip and hid her own bare, dirty hands in the folds of her skirts.

'You heard me,' the man answered, an edge of irritation lacing his tone.

The woman stilled and studied him. 'I do not believe you, brother.' Her voice dropped lower. 'Father was after you for years to marry, and you committed in an instant? To a woman you do not know, but met in the Grassmarket?' She scoffed. 'Doubtful. This is one of your ruses, and I will not fall for it.'

Catriona lifted her eyes and met the woman's light blue stare. When the woman said nothing, Catriona flushed and looked away.

Dash it all.

They spoke about her as if she weren't there or like she was a child, and they her parents.

Should she say something on her own behalf? But what exactly could she say? She frowned. Nothing that would make the situation any less ridiculous, and getting in between their sibling squabble seemed a poor idea. She had enough problems.

The dispute faded into silence as the carriage settled into a steady advance, moving in and out of the way as other carriages and merchants passed along the narrow-cobbled lanes of Edinburgh.

Catriona leaned against the cool wooden frame of the small window and stared out through the spotless glass. She'd never been in such a fine carriage, with its plush seats and dark stained interior. There was a heavenly hint of rose water, no doubt from the woman seated beside her. While she'd never been much affected by wealth or power, she had also never been so close to it. According to the exchange in the market, this man who had bought her was a laird. He'd spent a whole guinea on her. She'd never even seen a guinea in real life until today.

The man had means. Great means. If she hadn't been so terrified of the unknown, she might have allowed herself to sink further into the soft, voluminous seat and rest her eyes. But she needed to be alert and aware until she had more of an idea who this man was and what his plans for her were. She didn't dare meet the man's gaze despite the flood of questions assailing her mind.

What a fine mess Thomas had landed her in. Shame and anger heated her skin. To trade her away as if she was a mare without use, too old and weak to keep on because she had rebuffed his attentions this morn? Did she not have the right to choose what happened to her body despite his claims as her husband? Evidently not. Why could he not have merely abandoned her as everyone else that no longer wanted her had in the past? But this, being sold off to another man in the market square, was a new low in a long line of humiliations she had endured. Yet she would survive it as she had all the others before. She squared her shoulders and took in a breath. One day she would be free of all of this, just like Nettie always said.

Nettie.

Catriona missed the sweet old woman who had raised her in the small cottage off the coast of Lismore since she'd been lost at sea as a child with her parents never to be found. If only the dear woman had lived longer. Since Nettie's passing several years ago, when Catriona was only thirteen, she had worked as a servant on the island to the Chisholm family. When she turned nineteen, Thomas had come to her 'rescue', offered for her, and brought her to the city of Edinburgh.

Unfortunately, it turned out not to be a rescue after all, but servitude more than a marriage. Despite how she'd come to be in this carriage with this strange man and his sister, Catriona was grateful to at least be out of harm's way. This man didn't appear to be cruel. Although she'd thought that before with Thomas, hadn't she? She released a shuddering breath.

She rubbed her toe on the singular coin in her slipper to calm herself. A trick Nettie had shown her when she was a wee girl and afraid of everything. The cool feel of the worn threepence in the lining of her shoe was a reminder that she had been through worse and that she would survive this new development, no matter what was to be born of it.

'Child, ye canna go through the world afraid of yer wee shadow,' said Nettie as she ran her hands over Catriona's damp hair.

She sat curled in the woman's lap as she rocked back and forth in the fine carved chair her late husband had crafted from one of the trees from the glen. The fire crackled before them as the sun set off in the distance, bringing a glow to the small, cosy room.

'But Nettie, all I have in the world is you.'

'Aye. For now. But I will teach ye how to conquer yer fears and how to care for yerself, so when I am gone, ye will be strong and brave.'

'Will I learn to be fearless like you?' she asked, snuggling deeper into the wool folds of the blanket wrapped around her.

'Aye,' she whispered, pressing a kiss to her forehead. *'Ye will be braver than all of us. Ye survived a storm, remember? Any other lass would have drowned in those waters, but not ye. Ye washed up on my shore, strong and certain as if ye were meant to be there. Ye are a fine weathered stone capable of enduring anything, and don't ye forget it. The sun will shine on ye one day, and ye will be free and have all that was meant for ye.'*

But today would not be that day.

Catriona's body swayed with the carriage as it turned onto a lane taking them through the outskirts of the city.

Soon the tall, sharp edges of the buildings in the marketplace disappeared, and they headed through the heart of Edinburgh, away from the familiar sights, sounds, and smells of the city. Edinburgh castle loomed off in the distance. Its dark towers were a reminder of how small and insignificant she was.

It seemed she had escaped the clutches of one horrid man only to be placed into the hands of another. She pursed her lips. This man hadn't looked *too* horrid at first glance in the Grassmarket, but one could never tell, could they? Appearances were only that. What lay hidden beneath was what mattered.

She slid her eyes up to peer at the man through the curtain of loose hair shading her face, so she could study him without him knowing. He had short, straight, black hair, as dark as a raven's wing, and blue-green eyes the shade of a piece of sea glass she'd found once along the pebbled coast when she was but a child. His features were strong, but not sharp, and his form was pleasing enough. His dark fitted trews revealed his muscular legs, and the matching jacket with its fine silver buttons at the cuffs showcased his prominent shoulders as well as his wealth. She quirked her lips. He *was* quite an improvement from the smelly, flabby sot of a husband she'd woken up to this morn, but he was *still* a husband. As if she wanted or needed another husband, especially not one in such finery as this. No doubt he would be hard to please.

Despite being a laird—according to the man who'd almost bought her—he didn't have the arrogance of one. If anything, he'd been strangely kind, taking great pains to be gentle in removing the harness that Thomas had bound her in. Almost as if the laird was up to something. She narrowed her eyes as he sat stoic as one of the Standing Stones she'd seen once upon a journey with Thomas. Minutes of aching silence passed, and she wondered if they'd forgotten she was even there. She shifted closer to the door.

Perhaps they had.

They weren't moving terribly fast yet. If she acted now, she *could* jump from the carriage without much injury and disappear into one of the side streets. She was fleet of foot and always had been. Resting her hand on the door handle, she began calculating where they were, the best place to jump, and how fast she could run into hiding.

'I wouldn't if I were you,' the man stated.

Drat.

She released her hold on the handle, settled her hands back in her lap, and met the man's gaze: her new husband's gaze. His eyes didn't miss much, which would prove an added complication. She'd only share what was required of her until she had a better idea of just how quick-witted he was. Thomas was thick as a stump, which had been one of his attributes. One of the few.

'I am Ewan Stewart, Laird of Glenhaven,' the man offered. The tone of his voice rolled in smooth, deep waves, like the sea. 'This is my younger sister, Miss Brenna Stewart.'

She nodded. 'I am Mrs Catriona Gordon.'

'Mrs?' Miss Stewart asked the laird. 'I thought you said you found a wife.'

''Tis a bit complicated, sister. For now, you only need know that she will be our guest along our journey and at Glenhaven until our transaction can be sorted.'

'Transaction?' The woman's eyes widened more. 'What happened while I was in the milliner's store? I was not gone *that* long searching for a new hat, was I?'

Catriona pressed her lips together to smother a smile. If only she could speak so freely. All such direct talk had earned her in the past was a swift rebuke or an even swifter smack across the cheek.

This laird did neither. He was either a weak man she could walk all over or...kind. She wasn't entirely sure which was more unsettling. Time would tell as it always did, but she had plans to not be under his thumb for long, husband or not. It was high time she had her independence. Despite the longing she felt for Nettie and the family she had lost as a child, Catriona now yearned to be alone and free from the shackles of another's expectations and control. She wanted to live a life of her own choosing, and to finally ask herself what *she* wanted out of this world and have the quiet long enough to hear the answer.

'Where are we going, my laird?' she asked. Since he'd not answered his sister's enquiry, perhaps he might answer hers, since it required a much simpler answer. The sooner she knew their destination, the sooner she could begin crafting her escape.

He lifted his gaze to her once more. 'To our home in Argyll in the Highlands. We will stop at an inn in Glasgow tonight to rest, as the journey will take two days by carriage. We will arrive by nightfall on the morrow.' He muttered a curse. 'My apologies. Do you need to gather anything from your home? We can turn about and fetch your belongings before we travel further.'

'Nay,' she answered without a beat of hesitation.

He studied her, his brow furrowing. 'You have nothing you wish to retrieve?'

'What I care about I wear on my person. All else is replaceable.'

Miss Stewart smiled, her pale blue eyes as clear as the sky. 'We seem about the same size, Mrs Gordon. I am happy to provide you some gowns and such until the seamstress can make something to your liking.'

Catriona rubbed her hands together and swallowed uneasily. 'Thank you, Miss Stewart. That is very kind.' The offer was unexpected, so much so that she did not understand it or trust it, especially from a woman so pretty. She'd never found pretty women to be kind. If anything, they were cruel. But this woman seemed different, or perhaps just better at disguising her true self, much like Catriona was doing.

She stared out of the window and watched the city disappear into rolling hills and pastures. If she remembered correctly, Argyll was far north of here on the west coast.

'Have you any family we need send word to upon your arrival?' Laird Stewart asked.

Talk of family always turned her stomach. It would be far easier to lie, but she told him the truth instead, as it often brought any further questions to an abrupt end. 'Nay, my laird. I have been on my own since I was thirteen.'

'Is that how you came to be in such a position?' Miss Stewart asked.

'Sister,' Laird Stewart warned.

''Tis a fair question,' Catriona answered. She appreciated the woman's directness. 'Aye, it was. A woman without a dowry is not much use in the world, it seems.'

Although the woman didn't answer, the sympathy in her gaze stilled Catriona. Could she somehow understand her woes? She couldn't possibly. A woman of her looks and wealth? But as the woman's gaze fell away and her grip tightened on the reticule in her lap, Catriona wondered if being a woman of wealth and means was as limiting as being a woman of nothing.

Her stomach clenched, as she didn't wish to know the answer. Not now, as she travelled cross-country with a stranger who was now her husband to a place she had never been.

'When we arrive in Argyll, I will send word to our solicitor,' Laird Stewart began, staring down at a broadside in his hand. He paused. 'I am not familiar with the terms of our…arrangement. I want to have a better understanding of what your Mr Gordon was about this morning in the market. Never seen anything like it, to be honest. I still cannot fathom it is legal to buy a wife.' He folded the paper in half and tucked it within the pocket on the inside of his jacket.

She nodded. What did one say to that?

His sister balked. 'You bought her? You cannot *buy* a wife, brother.' She scoffed and shook her head.

'See for yourself,' he answered, handing her the broadside.

Miss Stewart read the paper. As she finished, her face paled to a stark, unnatural shade of white, and her mouth gaped open a bit. When she finally faced Catriona, her eyes were bright with unshed tears. 'I am sorry. I cannot fathom it.' She swallowed hard and reached out her gloved hand to gently take Catriona's filthy bare one. 'I am glad you are here with us. That Ewan saw fit to step in on your behalf.' She squeezed her hand briefly, and let it go before turning her gaze upon her brother. 'You are a good man, Ewan. Mother would be proud of you.'

He smiled back at her.

The affection between them made Catriona's gut twist. Such warmth thrust a distant memory of her own back to the surface. One of the few from her childhood. The laughter always came first.

'You must hurry... The waves come even now to crash upon the shore. We must chase them!' her eldest brother called to her and her siblings.

She laughed and ran after them, charging down the sandy shore deep into the dark waters, the coolness biting along her ankles and then her thighs. Soon she passed her sister and then her brothers. The water met her waist and then her chest, but she pushed on.

Her brother called out to her, and as she tried to turn to him, a roaring wave crashed over her head, swallowing her into silence. She fought against the waves as best she could, but the sea pulled her along as if she were a petal in the wind. Kicking her legs and flailing her arms, she tried to reach the surface for air, but the sea pulled her deeper and farther into its depths until there was only darkness.

'Mrs Gordon?'

Catriona looked up and met the Laird's gaze. 'Hmm?'

'Are you unwell?' he asked, his brow furrowing.

'Nay. I am fine, sir.' She lied.

He paused before nodding to her, a sliver of disbelief resting in his gaze. 'If you have need of anything along our journey let me, my sister, or our driver Aaron know. You are safe now.'

'Thank you,' she answered, knowing full well what could have happened if the other man had purchased her from Thomas. 'I am grateful for you stepping in when you did. The other man did not seem…as kind as you. I do not know what would have befallen me.'

A muscle flexed in his jaw. 'Nay. I wouldn't wish my worst enemy to the likes of MacGregor.' He shifted in his seat. 'And it gave me some sense of…relief to know that I had been able to help you when I wasn't able to do so before for someone I loved.'

Something heavy rested in his words. Perhaps a regret he wore close to his heart? A part of her softened at the sight of it. She gifted him a nod of understanding. She had a keen knowledge of regrets and what they did to a person.

Catriona stared back out the window, knowing full well she would not be there to hear the answers to any queries the laird sent out to his solicitors or any dressmakers' suggestions for new gowns. She would be gone as soon as she had some coin. It was just a matter of figuring out how to escape, where she would go once she did, and what new identity she would create. The possibilities seemed endless, and her stomach flipped with hope, a feeling she hadn't had in a long time.

This was her chance.

A life of freedom awaited her, and she would seize it. Nothing and no one would stand in her way. Not even a handsome and wealthy laird who might well be her new husband.

Chapter Three

Curses.

Ewan tugged at the cravat around his neck. Why had he not left it alone? Most likely Mrs Gordon could have cared for her own affairs. He could have done nothing, returned to his carriage, and been on with his day.

His gut twisted.

Nay. He couldn't have. Not when he had an idea of what would have happened to this woman if she'd fallen into the hands of MacGregor or some other unseemly character. While he'd not known about his older sister Moira's suffering at the time of her marriage and been able to prevent it, this woman was a different story. He had seen the abuse and danger she was in with his own eyes in the square. And he'd promised himself he'd step in if he ever saw another woman in such danger, just as he wished someone would have stepped in on Moira's behalf and saved her.

He'd done what he'd had to, but now what could be born of it? He needed a wife like he needed a swarm of locusts over his fields, especially when he didn't know if she was even his wife at all.

Yet again his emotion had ruled his mind and actions with rather dire consequences. His jaw tightened. Father was right. The Stewarts needed to be feared or else they might be conquered. If Ewan didn't begin to harness his feelings and emotions, all his 'care' for others would run the clan and his family's future adrift into the firth.

Perhaps he already had.

He glanced across the seat at Mrs Gordon with regret.

What fool bought a wife at market?

Evidently, he did.

The carriage was beginning to feel as snug as a coffin, and he couldn't escape the unease settling on him like a stone on his chest. Shifting further in the seats, he bumped the woman's knee as she sat across from him. 'My apologies, Mrs Gordon,' he murmured and shifted his leg away.

Her eyes flashed up to meet his briefly, and those amber irises arrested him once more, just as they had in the market. Such an unusual shade intrigued him. Hell, all of her did. He had never met a woman so at ease with the oddity of her situation. Most likely her nerves could withstand a battlefield. Her face was a mask, void of emotion. The only flicker of feeling he'd spied upon her face was in the brief moment before she'd admitted to having no family and having been on her own since she was in her teens. A glimmer of sadness had registered in her eyes before being hidden away under a cool nod as she had answered his enquiry and stared back outside the window.

Blazes. He ran a hand down his face. What would he do with her now?

The last woman he had spent any extent of time with alone whom he wasn't related to was Emogene. *Emogene*. He cracked his knuckles, and his throat tightened. Best he not think of her right now or he'd jump from this bloody carriage himself. He glanced up and met Mrs Gordon's assessing gaze. She was studying him for some reason. Could he blame her? She probably wondered if he would ravage her or throw her to the hounds upon their arrival at the inn. Of course, he would do neither, but she didn't know that. She didn't know him.

Just as he didn't know her.

'We will arrive in Glasgow at nightfall and secure rooms as well as food so that you are comfortable and cared for. And when we reach our home at Glenhaven,' he offered to put her at ease, 'I will ask our housekeeper, Mrs Stevens, to get you settled in one of our many guest chambers. She can also assign you a lady's maid to tend to your, erm…needs.' He tugged at the cuff of one of his coat sleeves. He was bumbling this miserably. 'And as my sister mentioned, she will find you some gowns you can borrow until a proper seamstress can be sent for to make you a wardrobe of your own. In due course, we will find out the legality of this marriage of ours and discuss the future.'

'Thank you,' Mrs Gordon answered, releasing a breath that caused her bosom to rise and fall against her rather drab and worn brown dress. The small silver chain of a necklace winked at him as it caught the sunlight. It led down her neckline but disappeared into her bosom, tucked away and hidden from view. He wondered what resided at the end of that chain, and why she took pains to hide it there.

When he glanced back up at her face, he was horrified to find she had noted the fall of his gaze. Pink flushed the apples of her cheeks and along her neck as she glanced away. *Blast.* And now he was an impertinent cad. He glanced outside at the rise in the terrain and spied the familiar outline of the city in the distance. At least they were not far from Glasgow. His lungs burned for fresh air, and his legs desired a reprieve from the cramped carriage. This simple trip to town for a few errands for his sister's upcoming nuptials had turned into quite the opposite.

He would return home with a bride.

The evening meal at the Black Lion Inn had been the usual hearty, but rather bland, fare of stew with bread and cheese often served at travelling inns such as these, but Ewan would not complain. Being out of the carriage with a full belly and a bed awaiting him one floor above was enough to make his heart sing. It had been a day he'd rather forget.

Mrs Gordon had quietly eaten, quietly talked, and quietly listened. Ewan wasn't sure what to do with her, but Brenna held the woman's subdued demeanour in stride by filling most of the silence with a running discourse of her own. To his surprise, Mrs Gordon seemed content to listen and smile and add in a quip or two.

After freshening up and draping one of Brenna's cloaks over her tattered and torn dress, Mrs Gordon blended in with them quite well. All in all, to an outsider the scene might look to be a small family gathering or a meeting of friends, not a woman who had just been bought for a guinea sitting with her new 'husband' and sister-in-law, if that's what they even were. Ewan blanched.

It sounded as bad as he thought it might in his head.

How in the world would he explain this to the leaders of the clan? To Moira? To Mrs Stevens? To the entire clan? His stomach churned with doubt.

Not well.

'How did you come to be in Edinburgh with Mr Gordon?' Brenna asked.

His sister's question piqued his interest. Mrs Gordon's answer might very well help him in explaining away the awkwardness to those who enquired.

Mrs Gordon set down her wine and cleared her throat before settling her hands in her lap. 'It is an odd story, really. I was raised by an older woman named Nettie on the island of Lismore from the time that I was six until she passed just after I turned thirteen. After that, I lived with the Arrans for a short time. Then, I worked as a servant to the Chisholm family. I truly believed that Thomas, Mr Gordon, was rescuing me from a rather squalid fate when he came to our small island on a fishing excursion and offered for me. I had no dowry and did not have any expectations for my future.' She bit her lip, and her gaze dropped away.

'May I ask what happened prior to staying with Nettie?' Ewan asked, his own curiosity getting the better of him.

'Nettie found me unconscious on the shore when she was out walking one morn, and brought me to her cottage to care for me. Said I slept for a full week before I woke, and could remember nothing of who I was or my family. I could not even remember my name or age, so she gave me the name Catriona and age of six, her guess as to how old I was.' She shrugged. 'Now I can remember that I had a family—parents and siblings—prior to living with her but no real details of who they were or my life before washing up on the shore.'

'Saints be. So, you had a family?' Brenna asked, her eyes wide in surprise. 'But you cannot locate them?'

'Aye. Nettie sent word out about finding me, but no one ever replied, and my parents never came for me. Over time, Nettie told me she believed they most likely drowned after our boat must have capsized at sea and that I was lucky to have survived.'

Her eyes told him there was far more to her history, but he'd not push her. They'd only just met, and she'd had quite the trying day, as they all had. He checked the wall clock and fought a yawn. 'May I escort you ladies up to your rooms? We have an early departure in the morn, so that we can reach Glenhaven by dark. Best we get some much-needed rest.'

'Thank you for the meal, my laird.'

'Of course, Mrs Gordon. 'Tis the least I can do after all you have been through today.'

And as he followed them up the stairs, he wondered

just how much more she had suffered and whether he wished to know the truth of it at all.

Catriona stared out her room window. She'd been up for quite some time after snatching a few hours of fitful sleep despite the soft bed and tidy accommodations the inn offered. It was dark, quiet, and perhaps the perfect time to escape. She looked at her empty room and felt around in her threadbare pockets. Perhaps not. How far would she get with no coin and no plan for supporting herself? She had no money except the threepence in her shoe and only the clothes on her back.

But…what if she waited until she reached Glenhaven to flee? The Highlands were more remote, with so many places to hide. She frowned. *If* you weren't found by the wrong person, that is. But she could manage that. Over the years, she had become adept at reading people's intentions, so she merely needed to trust her gut. She could make this work and be free at last. With some money, clean clothes, and some rest, she might just make a go of it.

She'd just have to keep her nerves and her wits about her until she had those things in her possession. The laird and his sister were kind, but they were not fools. They might expect her attempt to run. It was a good thing she had a day-long carriage ride to plan out her escape. She could close her eyes, feign sleep, and figure out all the details that she could. The laird and his sister had also told her a great deal about Glenhaven and the people and places within it, and most likely she'd learn more on the ride today. She could craft the layout of the castle and the list of what she would need in her head. Once they arrived, she could get clean clothes, eat, figure out where she could secure some extra coin and food, and be on her way. She could disappear into the Highlands, maybe even this eve, if all went to plan.

After an indecently long journey, Catriona woke with a start as she was jostled into Miss Stewart. 'Apologies, miss,' she mumbled, looking around her. The carriage lurched again as the horses pulled and began a steep ascent along a narrowing road. She glanced out of the window at the lush greenery and setting sun.

Blast. How long had she been sleeping? They were far from any city.

'We have almost arrived, Mrs Gordon,' said Laird Stewart as he met her fuzzy gaze. 'Only a few more minutes now and we will be at Glenhaven. I hope you will find your stay with us a comfortable one. As I mentioned before, Mrs Stevens will show you to your room and assign a maid to assist you.'

Before she could respond, the carriage rounded a turn, and a castle came into view, its tall sandy grey towers climbing high into the dusky sky and its arms spreading out far in the horizon.

Lord above.

So much for having already mapped the castle out in her head. She could never have imagined a place as great and looming as this. She'd never seen a castle so large. Well, except for Edinburgh Castle itself.

'Welcome to Glenhaven, Mrs Gordon,' he offered.

She blinked at this 'Glenhaven', unable to look away.

She commanded herself to at least close her gaping mouth, so she wouldn't look like a hooked fish pulled from the water, even if it was exactly how she felt arriving here after being plucked from the streets of Edinburgh. The fine estate rested atop vibrant green rolling hills and fields as far as she could see. Off in the distance there was what appeared to be a village to the south, the whitewashed cottages dotting the valley at intervals and disappearing down to what was most likely the banks of a river. She spied a large barn to the west, and several smaller workhouses, mills, and drying sheds to the east. *This* was her new life?

Perhaps Thomas wasn't such a bastard after all by gifting her this new life, even if he had sold her off like cattle.

A flicker of temptation to stay here as the laird's new wife snuck up on Catriona, but she batted it away quickly, fiercely. *Stay? Why ever would I stay when I could run and have a future of my own choosing at last?* Having independence and freedom would be worth far more than any luxury, wouldn't it? And she didn't even know this man. Nor did she know if this marriage was legal. He could be a horridly cruel master or a liar and a cheat. She met his half smile.

She furrowed her brow. Or maybe he was as kind as he appeared? *Dash it all.* What did one even do with a kind man? She had no idea. It would be easier if he were a brute. At least she knew what to do: stay out of the man's reach and tend to her own affairs. Mayhap it was the same with dealing with a kind man? Take care not to fall under the spell of false security, for happiness couldn't be trusted as it never lasted…or at least, it had never lasted for her. All those she loved she had lost somehow. By age, by nature, or by cruelty. She'd not fall for the idea of security again.

She was not born to the privilege of such certainty.

The carriage slowed to a stop in the drive, and Catriona's heart threatened to beat out of her chest. While she had been quite eager and ready to jump from the rolling carriage yesterday, now she was rather hesitant to leave its familiar confines. How did one even behave in such a place?

The driver jumped down from his box seat and opened the carriage door. 'Mrs Gordon?' he offered, extending a hand to assist her.

She swallowed hard, settled a mask of indifference on her face, squared her shoulders, and accepted his hand. What other option was there? She couldn't stay in the carriage with the hope of being forgotten. It was a trifle late for that.

As both of her feet settled onto the cobbled drive, she let go of his hand and breathed in the air of Argyll. A breeze ruffled her hair and kissed along her cheeks. Despite everything, she sighed aloud, enjoying the fresh air full of the crisp scent of new growth, as if one could smell the green of the grass. Not that one could. But she'd not smelled such fresh air in such a long time that her lungs savoured it.

The laird approached and offered his arm to her. 'Shall we?'

She pressed her lips together, uncertain of what exactly he had in mind, but she nodded and slid her hand into the crook of his elbow, acutely aware of the feel of his muscles beneath her touch.

They followed his sister inside, where they were greeted by a maid who offered to take their coats. Another servant gathered the parcels from the driver as he arrived behind them in the entryway.

'My laird, I trust ye had a successful outing.' An older woman greeted them as Catriona handed off her tattered shawl to a young maid, feeling nervous and exposed. The lass wore finer clothes than she. Catriona fiddled with the end of her torn dress sleeve as she awaited an introduction. No doubt she looked a mess and out of place despite her best efforts to hide her past. Her chest tightened. The memory of first being brought to a new home after Nettie died pressed upon her, and the same shame of such uncertainty made her fingertips tingle.

'Aye, we did. Thank you.' He straightened his cravat and faced the woman. 'Mrs Catriona Gordon shall be staying on with us awhile, Mrs Stevens. Could you provide her a lady's maid and whatever additional comforts she requires? My sister will be loaning her some gowns until a seamstress can be sent for, but before then, I would appreciate your assistance in seeing to her needs.'

The older woman nodded, only a small widening of her light grey eyes giving away her curiosity. To her credit, she asked no questions, but greeted Catriona with a warm smile and small curtsy. 'Welcome, Mrs Gordon. As the Laird stated, I am here to provide ye with whatever ye require.' The woman's soft smile put Catriona at ease, and she released a breath.

'Mrs Gordon,' the laird began. 'I will leave you to get settled in and rest before dinner. Does eight suit you?'

Did it suit her?

Catriona cleared her throat. 'Aye, my laird,' was all she could sputter out.

'Until then,' he replied and disappeared down a corridor with his sister not far behind.

'I'll send in one of our girls in shortly to assist ye, Mrs Gordon, but until then, let me take ye to yer room. I think the Goldenrod Room shall suit ye just fine.'

Catriona nodded and fell into step behind her, doing her best to slow their pace so she could take in the opulence and beauty of the castle. Rich, colourful tapestries hung from the walls amidst landscape paintings offset by the dark mouldings framing the walls and stone floors. The place was so large that their footfalls echoed with each step, and Catriona pressed her lips together to smother a bit of a giddy smile.

She was being ridiculous, of course. It was merely a castle, and she wasn't meeting the king or any such royalty. All the same, a flicker of joy filled her chest as they slowed and the maid... Catriona paused.

Was she a maid? Housekeeper? What did one call her?

Before she could land on one term of address, Mrs Stevens opened a door wide for effect. 'Yer chambers during yer stay here, Mrs Gordon.'

Catriona stood in awe. If she thought the hallways were glorious, this bedchamber, *her bedchamber*, was heaven itself. The room glowed in soft yellow hues. Not a loud noisy colour, but a light yellow like a buttercream set off with whites and subtle greens. In essence, she felt as if she were staring into a garden lush with blooms.

'I hope it is to yer liking?' she asked.

'It will more than do. It is beautiful.' Catriona couldn't tear her eyes away.

'Glad to hear it.' She paused. 'Do ye have any belongings ye wish to be brought in?'

Her words yanked Catriona back from her reverie, and she faced the older woman. 'Nay.' The single word sounded as final as it did tragic, especially surrounded by such opulence.

The woman's eyes softened. 'Aye. I'll send Betsy along with some fresh clothes for ye. Would ye like a bath drawn for ye to wash away yer journey?'

Did she?

Aye. More than she dared admit. She smothered a sigh at the thought of a warm bath. How long had it been since she had experienced such a luxury? She couldn't remember. 'That would be lovely. Thank you.'

'I'll see to it, Mrs Gordon.'

'Thank you.' Catriona fought the urge to grab the woman's hands and squeeze them within her own like she used to with Nettie when she was young and full of excitement. She clutched the folds of her skirts instead.

As the woman left, securing the door closed behind her, Catriona walked deeper into the large room and took it all in. There was a large, beautiful bed covered with plush, soft yellow bedding, a sizable wardrobe and matching dresser for clothes, a pale green sitting couch, and a small but tidy writing desk with a chair facing the outdoors. Sunshine beamed in through three small windows, the light bouncing off the bedding and the long flowing white drapes. A small potted plant with vibrant purple flowers bloomed in the corner of one window and winked at her from afar. While she had no idea of its origin, it was the perfect fit for the space with its double bloom dangling down the side of the clay pot.

She blinked. A harsher contrast to the living quarters she had shared with Thomas could not be possible. This room was spotless, full of light, quiet, and…peaceful. She sucked in a deep, greedy breath and closed her eyes, taking in the clean, crisp smell of laundered bedding, the faint remnants of polish, and the subtle sweetness of the blooms of the unknown plant in the room. Her room.

She opened her eyes. Even if she didn't stay long, she would revel in the peace this space offered her and pretend she was worthy of it. Their arrangement as his possible wife would be brief as she had plans to flee, but even a few hours of being the lady of the castle would be blissful. She'd never been the lady of anything. She'd never truly had anything except for the clothes on her back, the locket around her neck, the threepence in her shoe, and the thoughts in her head. All of this was quite overwhelming.

Realising she had at least a few minutes before the maid would arrive with her bath and clothes, she bit her lip, glanced back at the closed door, stripped off her tattered dress, stockings, and shoes, and gave in to the childish wish in her heart. She rushed over to the bed, dove onto its lush bedding with only her undergarments on, sank into the downy folds of material, and sighed.

Chapter Four

'Mrs Gordon?'

Catriona opened her eyes slowly, and then sat up with a start, her heart racing in her chest. She blinked and scanned the room. *Blazes*. Where was she?

The next thing she knew, a young maid was standing over her, a look of worry woven into her brow. 'Mrs Gordon?' she asked. 'Would ye like to take yer bath now, or shall I return with the water later?'

The girl appeared to be but a few years younger than Catriona. Her clear brown eyes blinked down at her in uncertainty. 'My apologies. I knocked, but when ye did not answer, I came in. I feared ye were unwell. Please do not be angry with me.'

'Nay,' Catriona answered, smiling at the girl. 'I merely fell asleep.'

Catriona hugged her arms to her chest as she realised she only wore her shift and had left a heap of dirty clothes on the floor. A blush heated her cheeks. 'My apologies, miss. I did not wish to soil the beautiful bedding.' She scrambled off the bed and onto the floor to gather the items she had so hastily discarded.

The girl rushed to her and began to take the items from her. 'I will get them for ye, Mrs Gordon. That is my job.'

Catriona stilled and pressed her lips together. 'I am sorry. I…' She faltered and let go of the soiled items and one of her worn boots as the girl gathered them from her and set them aside near the door.

The maid returned, no doubt as confused by Catriona's actions as she was. Catriona's shoulders slumped, and she risked the truth. 'I am not accustomed to being tended to.'

The girl smiled, revealing a dimple in each cheek. 'Then we shall get on well, Mrs Gordon. My name is Betsy. I have just started here as maid, so I am not used to how exactly to best serve ye.' She blushed and released a tentative laugh.

'Yes, we will be quite the pair. A lady unused to being tended to, and a maid unsure of how to tend.' Catriona could not resist joining in and allowed the first laugh to escape her body in quite some time. The release of the pressure of hardship, even if it was only for a few moments, felt almost as blissful as the downy bedding.

Almost.

'Shall I bring in the water for yer bath?' Betsy asked, her smile full and relaxed.

'Aye, Betsy,' Catriona answered. 'That would be lovely.'

She nodded. 'I shall be right back in. The tub is behind the wooden screen. Perhaps ye would like to select a soap?'

Before Catriona could enquire further, the slip of a girl was gone from the room. Select a soap? There was more than one? She approached the tall, decorative screen used for privacy for the bath. Walking on the smooth, clean wooden plank floor cooled the soles of her feet, and she paused for a moment. She could not remember when she had last dared to walk barefoot inside. One didn't walk about unprotected on dirty floors covered with refuse and vermin. She forced herself to remember she was safe here in this beautifully clean room and that she was awake. This was no dream. She shook her head, stepped around the screen, and spied a simple tub large enough for a soak. There was also a small table covered with soaps and bottles of what she could only assume were fragrant tinctures and mixtures for bathing. Again, she had little experience with such excess. She'd grown quite used to having one singular bar of soap, a cloth, and a basin to clean herself once a day if she were lucky. Baths were for the wealthy, not for the everyday person. Such water to waste was a luxury she'd never been accustomed to.

And you shouldn't get used to it.

For she wouldn't be here long. Not if she wished to claim her independence as she had always dreamed of. But it didn't mean she couldn't enjoy this one bath, so she would. Five shaped bars were laid out in an array before her on a small cloth. Lifting one to her nose, she breathed in deeply. Her toes curled and uncurled as the pull of soft lavender and sage filled her nostrils. Setting it down and lifting the next one to her nose, she smiled as the mixture of rose and dew greeted her. She smelled it again and sighed. The third bar smelled of sweet goat's milk and a summery floral scent, but she couldn't place the flower.

The door opened and closed. She set the soap back down and peeked around the screen, the thin strap of her shift sliding down her shoulder as she gripped the edge of the wood. Betsy walked slowly, the strain of lifting the large wooden bucket evident in her laboured gait. Catriona hurried around the screen and grabbed the handle to assist her.

'I may be new, but I am quite certain ye should not be helping me to make yer bath,' Betsy offered, even though she did not resist Catriona's help.

'Since I am unused to such pampering, I'm happy to assist you. I cannot remember the last time I had a hot bath.' She leaned her face over the steam rising from the contents of the barrel, basking in the bliss of warmth hitting her cheeks.

'I can say I have never met anyone like ye, Mrs Gordon, and we have only just met.' Betsy smiled, and together they carefully poured in the water.

'Nor I you,' Catriona answered, smiling back.

'There is another bucket outside.'

Another full bucket of hot water? Catriona could scarce believe it, but soon enough Betsy returned with another steaming barrel identical to the first and set it on the floor. She closed the chamber door and lifted the bucket. Catriona rushed over once more to help, and they giggled as they carried it over to the bath. They poured the contents in.

'Feel free to step in, my lady, and I will set this outside for the footmen to retrieve.'

Catriona removed her necklace carefully, setting it on the small writing desk. Then she walked back to the tub, cast her threadbare shift off to the side, eased her foot into the perfectly heated water, and sighed. Guiding her legs in one after another, she stood in the tub as the water warmed her, and then slowly sat, the water sluicing over her limbs, the heat so luscious she moaned aloud.

Betsy chuckled and appeared behind her. 'Is the bath to yer liking?'

'Aye,' she murmured as she closed her eyes and rested her arms on the sides of the small tub.

'I am glad of it. Have ye selected yer soap?'

She hadn't even finished smelling all of them, but on instinct, she chose the one that had stirred a flicker of interest in her as it was unknown. 'There was one that smelled of sweet goat's milk and some other flower I could not name. What is that one?'

Betsy smiled. ''Tis elderflower. A summer bloom. Ye may have seen them along the road. They have beautiful white sprays of blossoms. Quite delicate little things, but they smell divine.'

'Aye. Let us use that one.'

Catriona plugged her nose, dunked her head in the water, and emerged to hear Betsy's chuckle.

'I could have wet yer hair with the pitcher of water, my lady.'

'No need, Betsy,' she answered, wiping the water from her eyes. 'That was heavenly.'

'Hair first?'

'Aye.'

Betsy knelt beside her on the floor, scooped up her soaked hair, and began to work the soap into it until a lather formed. The feel of the girl's hands kneading Catriona's scalp felt blissful as the warm water relaxed her muscles and the sweet floral scent of the soap filled her nostrils.

Soon, Betsy set aside the soap. 'If ye'll sit forward and tilt yer head back, I'll rinse yer hair.'

Catriona did as the girl asked, and water cascaded down her hair and back once and then twice. Betsy squeezed the remaining water from Catriona's long hair and brought the heavy tresses forward to rest around her neck and down her chest. 'Ye have lovely hair, my lady. I have ne'er seen such a shade of—' Her words faltered, and a hitch sounded in the lass's throat.

Catriona moved further forward. 'Is that better?'

When Betsy didn't answer, Catriona turned to find the girl staring horrified at her bare back. Catriona flushed in embarrassment.

'I—I'm sorry, miss. I should not have noticed. I just—' She stammered out the apology but hesitated with the bar in her hand as she met Catriona's gaze. 'I do not wish to hurt ye.'

Catriona turned away. 'You need not worry, Betsy. Those scars have long since healed.'

On the outside anyway.

She shivered and pulled her legs up to her chest, wrapping her arms around them as she leaned forward.

Betsy tentatively rested the soap along the ugly

raised scars Catriona knew resided there and gently washed her back. It had been years since she had bothered to look upon them, and she had no wish to. The man who had put them there, Mr Arran, was the head of the first family that had taken her in after Nettie died. Although kind at times, when he drank, the man was prone to lose his temper.

As the eldest child in the household at thirteen, she had put herself in his path to protect the younger ones from his horsewhip. When she told a neighbour what he had done, the woman helped her secure work in the neighbouring village as a servant for a wealthy family, the Chisholms, where she stayed until she met Thomas. While Catriona was freed of his abuse, she often worried about the other children and the man's wife. She wished she had been able to save them, but as a lass struggling to survive herself, she had nothing to offer except some of the wages she sent back to them each month to help put food on their table and repay the kindness of taking her in after Nettie's death.

She could remember the feel of the lashings against her skin and the man's cruel words. *'Ye be nothin', lass. That's why yer parents never claimed ye.'* She closed her eyes to wish the memory away. It was a good thing she was leaving, and the laird would never have to cast his eyes upon them. No doubt he would be even more shocked and repulsed than Betsy.

Water cascaded down her back in two waves. 'I am sorry for whatever brought ye such, my lady. Ye seem kind to me. I am sure ye did not deserve it.'

'As you well know, Betsy, deserving is not always a qualification for such treatment from men.'

The girl paused. 'I do not know much about the ways of men other than my father and brothers. They are stern, but fair. Never once set a hand to me.'

The smooth soap slid down Catriona's arms, and the sweet smell and slight pressure loosened the discomfort in her chest. She stilled Betsy's hand with her own and met her gaze. 'Then you'd best keep it that way, you hear me?'

Betsy nodded. 'Aye, my lady.'

Soon, Catriona's hair was towel-dried and brushed, the gleaming light auburn locks almost unrecognisable as her own in the hand mirror. She shook her hair, gliding her fingers through the wavy, silky threads. Had she ever been this clean before? Every part of her skin seemed to shine and glisten as the sun set behind her. At a quarter 'til eight, Betsy entered the room with two gowns spilling from her arms. When she saw Catriona, the maid stopped short.

'My lady, ye are beautiful even without such finery,' she said as she gestured to the gowns she spread out on the bed.

Catriona shook her head. 'I do not recognise myself. I believe you have washed layers of dirt from me that I did not know I had, or perhaps there is magic in that goat's milk and elderflower soap.'

'Nay. Even I know there are no such magical soaps. Ye are a natural beauty.' She dropped her voice. 'I believe the men in this castle may trip over their own boots at the sight of ye.'

Catriona's throat dried. Beauty was not always an advantage, as it brought unwanted attentions. She had learned that from her first position as a young servant. *'Never be alone in a room with a man ye are not betrothed to,'* the older maids warned. And they'd been right. One of her fellow maids had been dismissed when she was found to be with child after being compromised by a young footman. It was one of the reasons Catriona had married young. She thought a husband would protect her and bring her respect in the world. Little did she know she would eventually need protection from him. She gripped the chair and placed the hand mirror face down on the dresser.

'I have two gowns from Miss Stewart. She picked them out with yer colouring in mind. What do ye think of them? Shall we try both?'

Catriona's stomach twisted as if she'd drunk goat's milk rather than bathed in it. She had no idea how to act at a fancy dinner such as this. She wrung her hands.

It is only one night. She could handle anything for one night, could she not?

'My lady?' Betsy asked.

'Both,' she sputtered out and rose, pasting a smile upon her face.

One night, one night, one night.

Then she would be free and on her own, travelling to a place of her choosing for the first time in her life. The thought sent a ripple of calm through her, and the nausea subsided. She finally looked upon the gowns Betsy had brought in, truly looked at them, and as her eyes settled on one, she could not deny her desire to wear it. 'The gold gown. There is no need to try on the other.'

She had never seen such a gorgeous gown in all her life, and if this were to be her only night to pretend to be a lady, a true lady, in a castle, then by all that was holy, she would enjoy it.

Betsy clapped her hands in glee. 'I had hoped ye would choose that one. I know just what to do with yer hair. Let us begin.'

Chapter Five

Ewan's stomach growled, and the mild irritation he'd felt at Mrs Gordon being a mere ten minutes late to their intended dining time was fast transforming into, well, something far worse. He sighed and shifted in his chair.

'Brother, you will not perish by waiting a few more minutes,' Brenna stated, trailing her fingers across the tines of her fork. 'Mrs Gordon has had quite a trying couple of days. Allow her some grace. I shall not bother to remind you how much of my life I have spent in the wings waiting for you or Father to come to some decision or another.' She smiled at him with the *you know I am right, so do not bother to refute me* look and head tilt that drove him mad. Then she settled her cloth napkin back in her lap.

The echoes of heeled footfalls sounded in the hallway, indicating Mrs Gordon's approach. 'Finally,' Ewan muttered and stood, sending a glare to his sister, who sent him a quelling look in return before giving a genuine smile to the woman who entered the room.

A woman Ewan did not wholly recognise.

Brenna warmly greeted Mrs Gordon and gathered her hands in her own, pointing out where she was to join her across the table. Ewan stood like an oaf struck dumb.

Blazes. By all that was holy, she was stunning, gorgeous even. A far cry from the tattered, broken woman he'd rescued.

She shone like a topaz, a fabled gemstone he had only seen in drawings. The gold gown, one of Brenna's, for he recognised it, looked joined with her flesh in a way he could never have imagined, and her pale skin glowed. Long, lush waves of her auburn hair cascaded down her back along with a crown of braids and a few loose strands that framed her face. His throat dried as the rest of his body tensed.

'My laird,' she greeted him as she rounded the table to her seat beside him.

He met her gaze and those familiar amber eyes. Then he regained his composure and half bowed to her before taking his seat. If her eyes had not been identical to those he'd seen before, he would not have believed this woman to be the one he met in the Grassmarket days ago. 'Mrs Gordon. You look lovely.'

'Thank you, my laird. I am grateful for your sister's kindness. Otherwise I would have had little to wear this eve.'

While her words were harmless on their own, Ewan shifted in his seat. The thought of her wearing 'little' sent his thoughts to rather devilish places.

She looked more than lovely. His words were a hollow attempt to remark upon her beauty, but his mouth seemed incapable of uttering a syllable more the longer he gazed upon her. Annoyed by his own weakness, he focused all his attentions on his napkin and the fine cutlery near his plate.

Deuces.

This was the absolute last thing he needed. Attraction led to nothing good, so it was best he smothered it entire. As their steak pies were set before them, he realised the appetite that had raged in his belly but moments ago had disappeared into nothingness while his utter awareness of her had surged in its place.

'And thank you for allowing me to stay here until I get my own affairs...tended to, my laird.' She cleared her throat, the meaning of her words not lost on him. The woman did not intend to stay, nor did he intend to ask her to. He had enough of his own affairs to sort out as the new laird. A fresh batch of correspondence as well as complaints from several of the clan leaders had arrived while he had been away.

'You may stay as long as you need, Mrs Gordon.' His words spilled from him before he realised what a terribly poor idea it was.

She nodded and released a breath. The relief registering in her eyes was unmistakable, and he felt like a cad. Perhaps the poor woman thought him as cruel as Dallan. Lairds did not possess the best of reputations for good reason, but he was not Dallan, nor was he the previous Laird of Glenhaven. He was trying desperately to be a good laird, one without regrets or distractions, and one who didn't rule by brute force or intimidation. But he also didn't want his emotions or attraction to this woman to cloud his judgement and cause a mistake like the one he'd blindly made with Emogene. A mistake that could cost the clan its future.

'Then, you are not married after all?' Brenna asked, her eyebrows arching towards her hairline.

Ewan rested his fork on the edge of his plate. While he adored his sister, at times she was as subtle as a rooster at dawn. He placed a mask of patience on his face. 'I am sure of little other than my uncertainty on the matter. I will send word to the solicitor in the morn to see what we can glean on the lawfulness of such an agreement. Until then, I cannot say one way or the other.'

'But you did buy her did you not? Is she not at least free from this Mr Gordon?' Brenna countered.

'Aye,' Catriona replied as colour filled her cheeks. 'He did, and I am grateful for it. I am hopeful I might buy my freedom from him or perhaps work off such a debt.'

'There is no need to discuss what we do not know. Let us simply enjoy the meal.' Ewan's words were tight and a touch too loud, but his message had been received.

Brenna smirked at him and set her sights on a new topic of conversation. 'Well, I am grateful you are here,' she told Mrs Gordon. 'It is far too serious in the house with just my brother and me here. Perhaps you can help brighten up this place.'

Ewan sighed and tried to remember to enjoy his food and not let his little sister's words prick him too much. Soon she too would be a bride and far from here, married to Garrick. And he would be all alone, which he didn't like to dwell upon at all.

* * *

Catriona thought not once, but twice about running her finger along the edge of her plate and bringing it to her lips to lap up every bit of the savoury sauce that remained. Had she ever eaten such a fine meal, and had her belly been so full? Nay. Did they eat this way each evening? She couldn't fathom it.

She gripped the napkin in her lap and commanded herself to keep her hands exactly where they were as her plate was cleared away. Soon a dainty little dessert was placed before her, and she almost squealed in delight like a child. It was a lovely cake covered in cream and berries. Her mouth watered despite her belly being full. The promise of sweetness the concoction offered threatened to consume all her reason.

Miss Stewart and Laird Stewart lifted their spoons, and Catriona did the same. When she raised the bite to her mouth, she closed her eyes as the sweet cream, cake, and berries burst into a perfect harmony of flavour. The next bite was exactly the same. Catriona listened contentedly as the siblings spoke of Miss Stewart's upcoming wedding without a care in the world, a feeling that was new and bewitching to her. She would savour their easy conversation like this dessert: for as long as it lasted.

Which, knowing her luck, wouldn't be for much longer.

She tried to push aside her worries and the knowledge that this was not a place she could or should stay for long. The laird might seem kind now, but she did not know him.

Had she ever really known anyone? Other than Nettie, not really. She'd moved too often or been too scared to tell people she met the truth about her past. Even Thomas hadn't known all of it.

She shoved away that thought too and scraped as much as she could from the bowl without drawing attention to herself.

'Do you know where your family was from, Mrs Gordon?' Miss Stewart asked.

Catriona stilled. It was a simple enough question, but she dreaded answering it every time it was asked. 'Nay. I am not certain. I cannot remember much of my childhood before being with Nettie.'

Too bad all the years after Nettie had died cut deep and sharp in her memories. Time had not dulled them.

'I am sorry to hear such,' Miss Stewart offered.

The laird sat silently. When she discovered him staring upon her scarred knuckles, she glanced away and tucked her hands in her lap. The familiar heat of embarrassment crawled up her neck and into her cheeks.

But she realised it was a bit late to hide the truth from him. He'd seen her shackled like an ox. Would anything shock him? For once, she'd not shy from it. She pulled back her shoulders and met his gaze while answering. 'I try to not focus on what I am sorry for, but what I have learned from all of those experiences.'

'Is that not but a way to deny it ever happened?' Laird Stewart asked. To her surprise, no challenge rested in his blue-green eyes, but a twinge of desperation to know the answer, as if he too had much invested in her next words.

So she chose them carefully. 'It could be, but I use what I have learned, despite how those lessons may have come about. Over the years, what I have realised from those many experiences has kept me alive.'

'Such as?'

'Such as me seeing you are desperate to know how I have survived thus far, but you are unwilling to ask me directly. Someone made you believe it was rude to be direct, but it isn't. Being rude is lying about one's intentions.'

He pointed to his chest. 'You mean me?'

'Do you think I do?'

He balked. '*I* have no ill intent. If anything, I saved you from peril with no thought to my own person or how this may further complicate my plans as laird.' He was flustered, so she nudged once more.

'Your eyes speak other words, my laird.'

He said nothing, and she had her truth.

And she'd gained the very answer she had wanted: the man had no bloody idea what to do with her. That was why he sat vexed and frustrated without finishing the food on his plate. He'd bought a bride he did not want and seemed altogether overwhelmed by his new role as laird. She almost felt sorry for the man.

But she didn't.

It was hard to feel sorry for a man who had inherited such power and wealth and yet had little idea of what to do with it. If *she* was in charge, she would have lists of ideas she'd attempt, and she would make no apologies for their successes or failings. She'd yield to no one... for once in her life.

'If you will excuse me, I have much to catch up on after being away for so many days.' Laird Stewart rose from the table, his gaze narrowing on her for a beat too long. Perhaps she'd overstepped a touch. She was his guest, after all.

She wrinkled her nose and brought herself back to reality.

She'd do well to remember her place. She was no laird, had no power, and never would. Well, not unless she seized it. She toyed with the napkin on her lap as she watched him walk away. But how did one do that with no money, no rights, and no hope for the future?

Simply answered: one didn't.

Unless the person was her.

This was her chance. She would not allow her one opportunity to seize the life she wanted to pass her by.

Chapter Six

'Where exactly do you plan to go, *wife*?'

Catriona froze at the threshold. Her hand grasped the door handle, a satchel stolen from the kitchen strapped to her back. Never mind the coin and food she had also 'borrowed' from the cook's coffers tucked inside it. There was no mistaking her purpose. She was fleeing in secret in the dead of night. It was as clear as the hard, chiding edge in the man's tone on the word *wife*.

Her hesitation was her downfall. If she'd but thrust the door open, she might have gained a start upon him and had a chance to disappear into the lush forest that whispered freedom across the edge of the large, empty fields. But now, with that beat of waiting, she had lost the option. Laird Ewan Stewart melted out of the shadows of the room. A slant of moonlight hit his blue-green eyes, and that flash of iris the colour of sea glass she'd noted on their first meeting sent a jolt of awareness and heat through her once more.

How did a man even learn to look upon someone that

way? She felt exposed and held all in the same moment. She shivered. It was wholly unnatural.

She leaned against the door, turning the handle slightly, and he ceased his advance, lifting an open palm in supplication.

'I mean you no harm,' he began, his voice softening to a rolling wave over her as if he was placating a small foal unknown to human touch. 'But I do wish for us to have one last conversation before you decide to leave.'

She turned the handle a degree more.

'Deuces. Just listen. I believe we may be able to help one another.'

Help one another? She almost snorted aloud.

What a farce. Or perhaps this was a finely veiled trap? She was a poor woman with nothing and no family to her name. He was a wealthy laird with power. While *he* could help himself to her, which is what one might expect from a man in his position, there was little she could offer him.

But even so, her curiosity at his play of words intrigued her, and he could have already lunged and pinned her to the ground if he'd wished to. He was no small man, and he had quick eyes. He didn't seem to miss much, which was becoming quite the nuisance. Dim-witted men suited her far better. This one was, well…quite peculiar. She couldn't sort him out at all.

She held his gaze, studying him. He was a puzzle amongst men.

No deception rested in his eyes, and she knew people. It was one of the things that had kept her alive for so very long. Being able to read them and foresee their intentions had spared her life on more than one occasion.

She let go of the door handle. Her instincts had kept her alive this long, so she'd trust them again now. 'Go on,' she replied, ever watchful for any unexpected movements.

'What is it you want, Mrs Gordon?' he asked.

What do I want?

She balked and narrowed her eyes. 'What?' she asked, shifting on her feet.

'You heard me.' His voice was steady, clear, and certain. The very opposite of how she felt at this moment.

It had been so long since anyone had asked her what she wanted that she was flummoxed to think of an answer. She sputtered out the first word that formed in her heart, 'Freedom.'

He lifted a brow and nodded. 'Not exactly what I thought you might say.' He crossed his arms against his chest. 'But I still believe we may be able to help one another.'

'Why should I help you with anything?' She bristled. 'I can still run from here.'

'Aye,' he answered, his gaze sweeping across her form with approval. 'You seem strong and capable enough. I believe you could survive…for a time. But for how long would a woman such as yourself be able to travel alone through these parts safely?'

He had a point, and it plagued her to concede it, so she refused to. 'I could make it.' She lifted her chin and squared her shoulders to rally her full height, no matter how meagre it was.

A smile tugged up the corner of his lips. 'I have no doubt as to your will. It is the will of others I would not trust. As you well know, not all men are kind.' His smile fell into a flat line.

A shiver scurried up her spine.

'And what are you, then?' she asked quietly.

He paused. 'What do you believe I am?'

'I believe you are like most men. It depends on how you need to be. You can be kind, but also cruel.'

To her surprise, he didn't become angry, but nodded in agreement.

'Aye. Quite right. I possess the duality of most men, but I believe my actions at the Grassmarket might earn me at least a listen.' He came closer, his steps measured and precise like a man trying not to startle a grouse in the brush. He paused an arm's length from her. 'But first, I would have you set down your satchel, or shall I say the cook's satchel, so I know you will stay long enough to hear out my proposal.'

She blushed. 'I would have returned it…someday.'

'No doubt. I have her to thank. She noted it was missing along with a few coins meant for the deliveries arriving tomorrow.'

Blast. Catriona's shoulders slumped. No wonder she'd been caught.

He reached out an open hand to her slowly and paused before touching her, staring into her eyes while awaiting her approval. She gave a nod, and he slid his hand under the worn leather strap of the bag, the heat from his fingertips seeping into her shawl, igniting a small trail of awareness along her shoulder and arm as he slid it away from her to rest at her feet.

She swallowed the nerves fluttering in her throat. He was close. Too close. She could see the fine shape of his jawline and the soft shadow of stubble on his cheeks. His slight scent of mint tickled her nose.

Her heart picked up speed. He swallowed, his Adam's apple bobbing in his throat, as if he were not entirely sure of his words even as he began to speak them. 'If we are not legally married by this transaction of ours, stay and be my wife. I know it seems an unusual request since we know so little of one another. But I think such a union could benefit us both. I need to solidify my new standing as laird, but I have no desire to go through the manoeuvrings of the clan leaders to find a bride. And in return, I could grant you security, protection, and immense freedom to pursue your interests as you desire. I saw the way your face softened at the sight of the clarsach and pianoforte in the salon. Whether your interests lie in music or art, it makes no matter to me. And once enough time had passed and you felt comfortable, er, with me...we could begin the task of begetting an heir.'

She blinked back at him. 'What?'

He chuckled, a deep smile brightening his features. A hidden dimple emerged and winked at her. Her heart skittered in her chest.

'You heard me.'

'But you own me already, my laird. You could just seize me now. I am at *your* bidding.'

He shook his head and took a step closer.

'Nay. I know you do not know me, Mrs Gordon, but

I am not that man.' He lifted one of her hands in his, running the callused pad of his thumb so gently over the small scars that covered her knuckles that she almost gasped aloud. 'I do not pretend to know what has befallen you.' He let go of her hand once his thumb reached her fingertips, and her breath hitched in her chest. 'But I will not add to it.'

She stared into his face, looking for deceit, but only truth shone back at her.

'So, you would just let me leave?' Surely she had misunderstood.

He shrugged. 'Aye. If you so wish it.'

'Why?'

'Because I do not own you despite this foolishness of the guinea at the Grassmarket. I just wished to save you from further injury and acted impulsively. I had not a thought past that moment of liberating you from your husband and MacGregor.' He ran a hand through his hair. 'And, I have no desire to own you. My offer to you now is one of partnership that would benefit us both. You could be safe, settled, and have all you require to live a good life here at Glenhaven, and you would assist me in being my wife to help solidify my standing as the new laird. Things are quite precarious at the moment.'

'Why not merely marry one of the many lasses who no doubt fall like petals at your feet? As laird, the men of the clan must have their daughters fawning about you and clamouring for your hand.'

'Aye, but that is the problem. I have no time or talent to manage such manoeuvrings, and I am uncertain of whom to trust, especially with the balance of power so in flux amongst my late father's friends. I believe some of them wish I were not laird, and some of them might well wish me dead, if I am to be entirely truthful. You would come to me with no ulterior motives and no expectations.'

She lifted her brow.

He shrugged. 'Aye, perhaps *fewer* expectations.'

'And your expectations of me?'

'As I said, assist me in solidifying my position as laird, help me root out any men with unsavoury intentions within the clan, and take part in begetting an heir, when the time is right. Oh, and our marriage will be an arrangement free of the entanglements of romantic love and that nonsense. I need no further complications in *that* area of my life. This would be a marriage of convenience for the both of us. Nothing more.'

A muscle worked in his jaw, and a coldness came into his eyes, darkening his features. The sudden change in him was stark and unsettling. *Dash it all.* A woman had hurt him. And deeply. That much was clear to see, but it made no matter to her. She was fine without love. She'd never experienced it, so why worry over it now? And she found him attractive. Much more so than Thomas. It might not even be a trial to endure his attentions in the siring of that heir of his.

But she'd not give in just yet, not when she clearly had the advantage for once in her life. 'And my allowance?'

He smiled. 'What is the monthly sum you require?'

'Five shillings.'

He pressed his lips together and sighed as if deciding whether he could agree to such an exorbitant amount.

'Done.' He extended his hand to her. 'We have an agreement, Mrs Gordon.'

She smiled and clutched her hand in his. 'Aye. Perhaps we could address one another by our given names now, since we are to be husband and wife after all.'

He drew his hand away slowly, and his smile faltered on his lips. 'Aye. Catriona, we can.'

Her name on his lips sounded forbidden, and her pulse increased. She longed to hear it again. A skitter of uncertainty clogged her throat. Had she just made an agreement with a saint or the devil?

Only time would tell, as it always did.

'May I escort you back to your room?' he asked.

'No need. I won't flee, but I'd like to sit and enjoy the view for awhile.'

He nodded. 'It is gorgeous.'

'Aye.'

'Until tomorrow then,' he said.

She faced the rolling hills, the moonlight glistening off the dark grasses bending in the breeze.

'And, by the way,' he called back to her.

She glanced around her shoulder and met his playful smirk and rogue dimple.

'I would have given you ten,' he said.

She shook her head as he continued, disappearing around the corner until she was left with only the small satchel, which she'd need to return to the cook with a hefty apology, and the view of a place that would now be her home.

While she'd woken up with plans to flee to seize her freedom, she was going to bed tonight in Glenhaven as the wife of a laird with the promise of more freedom, security, and protection than she'd had all her life.

Chapter Seven

Deuces.

By all that was holy, what had he just done?

Ewan scrubbed a hand through his hair and blew out a breath before he closed the door to his chamber. Had he made the best or worst decision of his life by making such a proposal?

His hands trembled as he leaned back against the solid wood of the door, the firm pressure a reminder he was alive and what he'd just done had not been an imagining. Mrs Gordon, Catriona, had agreed to stay and be his wife. And despite the utter panic he felt now, his desperation at the sight of her perched at the door ready to flee had been a thousand times more potent. His limbs tingled from the memory. All he knew was that he couldn't let her go.

Had he acted on instinct and done what he needed to do to keep her safe, just as he had at the Grassmarket, for fear of what might happen to her if she charged off into the Highlands alone at night? It felt like something more had sent him into such a state, but he cared not to acknowledge it. Perhaps it was just lust or attraction that had propelled him on so fiercely and with such certainty. He'd just reacted. He'd thought of nothing else but keeping her from leaving him…but why? He hardly knew the lass. But what he knew of her, he was drawn to, intrigued by, and it had been a long time since any such interest had flickered in him since Emogene.

And as much as he didn't want to say it, he was over-whelmed by the prospect of being alone at Glenhaven after Brenna married, and tackling the sea of decisions being a laird entailed. If only Father had told him how difficult it would be to fill his shoes.

Pushing off the door, Ewan rolled his neck and walked over to the bank of windows that overlooked the glen. He could see as far off as the moon and moun-tains would allow. The sharp and subtle bends of grey and black amongst the moonlight were as familiar and clear as the lines on his palms.

'That is Stewart land.'

Laird Bran Stewart rested his hands along Ewan's shoulders, and Ewan stood on his tiptoes to spy over the lower window frame.

'How far does it go, Father?'

'As far as you can see, son, and in time it will all be yours. Yours to care for, lead, and bring to greater prosperity.'

'It will?'

'Aye. Once I am gone, it will be your responsibility to care for our people, our land, and the fruits of it, for one day you will be laird.'

'How will I know how to be the laird?'

Laird Stewart released a deep laugh. 'Because I will teach you. The rest of it was sewn in your bones the day you were born to this world.'

'What if I don't want it sewn in my bones?'

'What you want doesn't matter, son. Your duty to the clan is above all else. Do you understand?' His father's voice was stern and unyielding.

'Aye, Father.'

But in truth, Ewan hadn't understood. He never had. His bones hadn't been filled with the duty and knowing of a laird, but with uncertainty laced with doubt. He shifted on his feet. But there was only one way through his choices now, and that was forward. He'd not go back on his word to Mrs Gordon. To Catriona. He swallowed hard and ran his hand through his hair. He knew far too well what the consequences could be from breaking one's promises. When Ewan had broken his promise to marry Robertson's eldest daughter in order to marry Emogene, an alliance was lost, his relationship with his father and clan fractured, and when Emogene left him in the end, Ewan's heart and belief in love were shattered. He'd sacrificed all for nothing.

He clenched his fists by his sides, let out a steadying breath, and headed over to his desk. Brooding was a waste of time. Perhaps one of the few things he and Father had ever agreed upon. Lighting a candle from one of the winking wall sconces, he settled into his worn desk chair. He found fresh parchment and his ink pot and quill. Enquiries would have to be made to find out the legal manoeuvrings of his agreement with Mr Gordon over Catriona. Best to know what would need to be done to ensure she was truly legally free of her husband before Ewan attempted to claim her as his wife in public.

As he ended the first word with a flourish of his quill, he settled into the rhythm of action, and some of the uncertainty from earlier melted out of the ink and onto the parchment. Action always soothed him far more than worry ever did.

A small knock sounded on his door.

Saints be.

Could he not have more than a handful of minutes of peace?

'Brother?'

Apparently not.

'Come in, Bren,' he called, knowing full well he'd not latched his door. He never did. Perhaps he should.

He set the quill back it its pot and rose as his sister entered the room. Worry creased her usually perfect brow. He prepared himself. Bad news had been the norm.

She settled into the chair near the window, tucking her legs under her and fidgeting with the tail of the tie of her cream dressing gown.

'Has something happened? 'Tis quite late.' he said. He was reluctant to sit. He preferred to stand for bad news.

'Nay, but I cannot sleep. When I saw the candlelight beneath the door, I decided to just come ask you about my worries.'

'Worries?'

'What are you to do…with Mrs Gordon? Surely

you will not send her away after all she has suffered.'
Brenna met his gaze, her eyes flashing with concern.

'Of course not. I said as much at dinner, did I not?'
He widened his stance and crossed his arms against
his chest.

She shifted and rolled her eyes heavenward. 'Aye.
I know what you *said*, but is that what you will do?'

'Is there oft a difference?'

She lowered her gaze. 'Aye. Sometimes there is.
Your…opinions—' she paused '—are not always fixed.'
She straightened her robe around her slippers.

'What does that mean?'

Silence.

'Bren?'

She huffed, but finally answered. 'You are often in-
fluenced by Father's friends and trying to be the perfect laird since Father passed, as if there is even such a
thing, and I wondered what you might do if they said
they disapproved of her staying on until she found
another…opportunity.' She locked on his gaze.

'I am in the midst of drafting enquiries as to her
situation to see what legal grounds there are for ensur-
ing she is legally free from her husband. I assure you,
I will not merely toss her out into the glen.' He set his
hands to his waist and walked to the window. His pulse
picked up speed. 'That way I will know when I can
marry her properly.'

There. He'd said it aloud and to Bren. There was no
taking it back now. It might as well be etched in stone.

When she said nothing, he turned to face her. Her
piercing blue eyes searched his as they often did when

she wished to assess his sincerity. She stood and walked to him. 'You are serious?'

'Aye. I would not joke on the matter of marriage, as you well know.'

'Do you love her?'

'Of course not. I barely *know* her, Bren. I met her in the Grassmarket a mere few moments before you did,' he scoffed and shook his head.

'Then, why on earth would you be wanting to marry her?' His skin heated under her scrutiny. 'She is not to be trifled with, brother. The woman has been through enough.' She frowned at him, crossing her arms against her chest.

He lifted his palms in supplication. 'I am not trifling with her. I proposed to her, you fool.'

She froze. 'Why?' she asked in a raised voice.

'*Because* I do not love her, and she comes to me with few expectations, unlike everyone else in my life. I will not have to endure the endless manoeuvrings of the elders and Father's most dear friends as they thrust their beloved available daughters upon me. And I will be free of your scrutiny as well as Moira's, for I will have finally taken a bride.'

Her pained expression told him his words had hit their mark, even though he hadn't meant to be quite so forceful in making his point. As she studied him further, her expression softened.

'Do you mean our care and concern for you?' she asked. 'For that is what it is, brother, not scrutiny. We have been worried for you since Father's passing. You put so much pressure upon yourself to solve all the problems of this clan. You hardly sleep, from what I can tell. You overwhelm yourself and think all must be resolved, but there will be new issues to address. That is the way it always was and will be.' She approached him and took his hands in her own cool, petite ones. He commanded himself not to pull away, despite the discomfort in his chest and emotion clogging his throat.

'The confidence and joy you once had seems to have been buried with Father, and neither of us know why. He is not here judging you, nor are we. We are your family. We care for you and wish you every happiness. And choosing Mrs Gordon as a wife because you do not know or love her seems a poor choice.' She squeezed his hands, and after a beat he pulled away and turned away from her.

Anger simmered in his blood. 'You do not know what is best for me. No one does. I am laird, and I will make the decisions for this clan and for myself.' He turned to face her.

She held her ground. 'So we should merely stand by and allow you to make yourself more and more miserable?'

'I am not making myself miserable.'

'Oh, no?' She popped her hands to her hips. 'You rarely laugh or have fun anymore, Ewan. You have become some serious facsimile of Father.'

'Nay. I have not.'

She scoffed. 'Then I will leave you to it, my laird. But do not come to me in a month's time asking for advice on how to undo the tangled web you have woven. By then, it will be far too late.'

'Do not fear it, sister. I won't.'

And with that, she glared at him and left the room, closing the door rather loudly behind her.

He cursed and scrubbed a hand through his hair. Why was everything so difficult? Couldn't one thing be easy? He thought of Catriona. Aye, having her as a bride might be just that—easy. She seemed an intelligent, sensible woman who was not afraid of hard work or difficulty. But first, he had to ensure she was legally free from her first husband, and Ewan could only do that by finishing the enquiry letter to his solicitor that he had intended to finish a half hour ago. He cursed once more and set down to task, his quill striking the parchment with a violent flourish, snapping the fine tip in half.

Chapter Eight

Catriona awoke in a plush armchair. She squinted against the striking rays of dawn streaming into a set of sizeable windows overlooking the glen. A light fog hovered over it, and the sunrise burned an orange pink in the distance. Unsure of where she was, she started, and half fell out of the plush cushions but recovered before she ended up on her backside on the floor. Her heart raced as she studied her surroundings, sitting on the edge of the chair, gripping the solid, steady arms of it fiercely. Finally, the memory of where she was clicked into place, and she sighed.

She was safe. She was at Glenhaven.

She froze.

She was also engaged to the laird even though she might be still married to Thomas. She groaned aloud and flopped back into the chair. She didn't know what anything meant any more. The only thing certain was that the days would climb on one way or another. The sun would always rise, the sun would set, and day and night would rest in between. It always had, and it always would. What she did with those days was the uncertainty.

Although being married to a laird might bring her more security and safety than she had ever had before, the freedom he promised was more of a question mark. She had never known a man who encouraged a wife to have freedoms.

Only time will tell, I suppose.

'Mrs Gordon?'

Catriona bolted to standing and whirled around, her arms high to protect herself.

Betsy, her lady's maid from the night before, stood wide-eyed like a deer surprised in the wood by a foe.

Catriona relaxed and dropped her arms to her sides. 'My apologies, Betsy. You gave me a fine start.'

'I am sorry, Mrs Gordon. I came to yer rooms with yer morning basin of water, and when ye weren't there, I started to worry for ye. I went looking to see if ye had need of me. Did ye sleep out here all night?'

'Aye,' Catriona answered. 'I was watching the stars and...' She shrugged.

'Fell asleep?'

'It appears that way. I am sorry you keep finding me asleep in the oddest places.' She covered her mouth as she yawned.

Betsy smiled. 'Ye had quite a journey the last few days, so I'm not surprised. Would you care to freshen up and dress? I can even bring ye a tray to break yer fast if ye wish.'

She smiled and released a breath. 'Aye to everything.'

Catriona completed her ablutions and dressed quickly with Betsy's help. With her stomach now full, she wondered what to do with her day. She couldn't remember the last time she had not a task or a chore to complete. Betsy had chided her more than once to stop doing her work, but being pampered was an odd, foreign feeling, and restlessness bubbled in Catriona. What did a woman do if she had no chores? She worried her hands. What did she *want* to do?

It had been a long time since she had asked such a question of herself, let alone answered it. She quirked her lips and wandered through the castle, nodding to the many servants as she passed, until she found herself near the salon the laird had shown her the night before. She peeked into the room with its muted hues and gentle floral accents that offset the dark, rich wooden flooring and decorative rugs. It was an invitingly feminine room, and she risked one step and then another across the threshold.

Once inside, she smiled as she scanned the room. Off in the corner sat a glorious wooden clarsach on a rose-coloured fabric-covered stool, and her fingers itched to play it, despite having no idea how. Just the thought of hearing music soothed her as it always had. Nettie had a lovely singing voice and often sang her back to sleep when she had nightmares. And more than once she had stood at the edge of the ballroom, watching the musicians play and tapping her toes to the music between serving wine and food to those who attended the seasonal balls at the Chisholms', where she had worked as a servant.

Perhaps she could sneak in just for a moment. It was early yet, so she'd need to be quiet. She closed the door behind her and prayed she wouldn't wake anyone else

in the household as she didn't know if she was even allowed to roam so freely.

Thankfully the sound of her footfalls was swallowed
up by the large rug that covered most of the floor. Her
fingers tingled in anticipation as she approached the
small harp, and once she reached it, she stopped, ad-
miring the delicate floral carvings that curled along
the triangular-shaped wooden frame and fine strings
beneath. She picked it up and settled onto the stool,
resting the clarsach on her lap. She ran her index finger along three of the strings, and they sang in delight
as if they were also longing to be touched. She smiled
at the sweet sound and did it once more but included
five strings along the run. It sounded even more glorious. She bit her lip and dared run her fingertip along
all the strings, and it sounded like a sunset in her ears.

'Do you play?'

Catriona stilled. *Laird Stewart.* While she'd only
known the man a few days, she knew that voice. Too
bad she didn't know him well enough to judge his tone.
She wasn't sure if he was angry or intrigued to find her
in the salon.

She turned to face him, stunned by the difference
in his appearance from yesterday. He stood in sandy
trews with high boots and a freshly starched cravat, but
no jacket. He appeared more relaxed and at ease, even
though he looked just as formidable as always as his
form filled the doorway. She met his gaze and risked
a light tone. 'Nay, but I would like to one day learn.'

'Does today suit?' He smiled and tucked his hands
in his trouser pockets.

She balked, surprised by such an offer. 'Today? As in this minute?'

He shrugged. 'Why not? My sister is convinced I am too serious and having no fun as of late. 'Tis early. I am not needed yet.'

She studied him. 'You play?'

'I do.'

His simple answer threatened to bring her flat to the floor. A laird who played the clarsach? It sounded near impossible, but the last few days had been nothing but one impossibility after another, had they not? Why should today be any different?

'I will take your surprise as agreement to begin your first lesson.'

She nodded.

'May I?' he asked as he approached.

She started to get up from her seat, but he shook his head. 'No need. I can guide you from where you are sitting.' He pulled up another stool and settled in beside her, his knee lightly bumping her own, sending a tiny current through her thigh.

'We shall start with something simple,' he said. His muscular frame filled the space between them as did his familiar scent of tallow, mint and something she couldn't quite name.

She watched him in awe as his large hand made the harp sing sweetly in what appeared to be an effortless rhythmic stroke of his fingertips across the first, third, and then fourth strings in a repeated refrain.

'That was lovely,' she told him.

'Now you try.' He handed her the small harp, and

she settled it in her lap. A flash of his rogue dimple appeared and disappeared just as quickly as if it was flirting with her.

Confidently, she sat up straight and did exactly as he did, but it sounded horrid. She cringed.

'May I?' he asked, reaching for her hand.

She hesitated but finally agreed with a nod.

He cupped her hand in one of his own and guided her fingers near the instrument. 'Try keeping your thumb pointed up to the ceiling and using just the pad of each of your first three fingers here to pluck the strings,' he said, tracing the plump part of her fingertips with the thumb of his other hand. Shivers scurried along her skin from the heat and intimacy of his touch, and a dull ache pooled in her core.

'Try again,' he said, undeterred, as if that hadn't been the most unpleasant music he had ever heard.

She swallowed the tightness in her throat and nodded. Taking a breath, she floated her fingertips along the strings again, and…it sounded even worse. *Ack.* Heat filled her cheeks. 'You make it appear quite easy when it is not.' She tucked a loose lock behind her ear and bit her lip.

'*That* is the first lesson of the clarsach,' he said lightly. 'Playing the harp is *never* as easy as it looks.'

She laughed aloud. 'Perhaps. Who taught you to play so well?'

His smile faltered. 'My mother. She was an incredibly talented woman. Her music and laughter used to fill these halls, especially this room. She could play the clarsach, the pianoforte, and even sing while playing and not miss a note.'

Catriona scanned the room imagining just that. A woman playing while the laird, Ewan, and his siblings danced with a fire blazing in the hearth. Her eyes paused on a large portrait of a fair-haired woman with rather delicate features across the room.

'Aye.' He nodded, reading her thoughts. 'That is her.'

'I like her smirk,' Catriona added.

Ewan chuckled. 'She had a glorious sense of humour, but she could also quell us all into silence with a single lift of her eyebrow, even my father.'

'Sounds like a magnificent woman, to be sure.'

'She was, and we were shocked when she died suddenly. In this very room, actually,' he added without her enquiry. 'Her heart just gave out. I have not been in here in far too long.'

'Why not?'

He shrugged and looked about. 'Too painful, I think. It was as if she took all the laughter and light with her that day. Being in here was a reminder of that. We plodded along as best we could, but it was never the same. I always thought it affected Moira the most, but now I realise it was Bren who suffered deeply. Turned herself inside out to be loved and pleasing, especially with Father.'

'And what of you?'

'Me?' he asked. 'I just miss her and the way it used to be. Of what could have been if she were still here. The conversations we might have had.' He gazed down at his hands. 'It is hard to think she has been gone over ten years.'

She could imagine him now, not as the strong, vibrant laird he was now, but as a younger, dark-haired lad sitting in this very room, having lost his mother, staring upon her portrait in silence. 'I am sorry. That must have been difficult.'

'It was, but it was perhaps a far cry from your own difficulties.' He ran his hands along his thighs and studied her face again with those deep, penetrating blue-green eyes that made her feel cared for and exposed all at once.

She looked down and toyed with the chain around her neck. 'It is hard to miss what one cannot remember. Not truly remember, anyway.'

'I doubt that.'

The truth of his words stung her, and her breath caught. She glanced up to find him assessing her once more.

The clock chimed, revealing the turn of the hour.

'Ah, the morn is getting away from me already. I will leave you to practice,' he said, rising from the stool. 'Just keep running your fingers along those first few strings to get the feel of it. Once you have mastered that, I will show you another note.' He nodded to her. 'I will be meeting with some of the clan leaders this morn, but I will try to find you later to give you the grand tour of the place. If you have need of anything, let Mrs Stevens know.'

'Aye,' she answered, unable to utter anything else. Then he was gone.

Dash it all. She felt entirely unnerved and intrigued by the man all at the same time. She scrunched up her face. *How odd.* Men usually didn't make her feel much of…anything. She shrugged off her wonderings and looked upon the small harp in her lap.

Her fingers drifted across the strings just as his had, and she cringed. It still sounded horrid. Staring down at her hands, she wondered how a man such as him, a laird of a clan, had made the strings of this clarsach sing so pleasantly under his touch?

Probably the same way he had made her skin sing. Frowning, she set aside the harp on the other stool, then shivered and rubbed her arms. Best she remain watchful and alert, and keep her distance until she figured this man out. There was no need to care more for him more than she needed to. While she might have agreed to become his wife, she intended to enjoy her freedom for the first time in her life. She also needed to keep her part of their bargain: there would be *no* romantic complications.

Chapter Nine

'What has you smiling this morn, brother?'

Brenna's question yanked Ewan from his thoughts as he walked down the main hall to his study, where three of the clan leaders would soon be joining him. Immediately he frowned and squared his shoulders, preparing for whatever his sister dared say next, which could be anything.

'What do you mean?' he countered.

She fell in step with him, matching his stride. 'I saw you. You were smiling as you were walking down this hallway.' She glanced behind them, curiosity evident in her tone. 'From whence did you come?'

He rolled his eyes and ignored her, unwilling to give away any of his thoughts regarding why he might be smiling, if he was at all, because of their talk the night before. Her doubt as to his intentions with Catriona still stung. 'Do you not have more pressing matters today to attend to? A fitting? Correspondence perhaps?'

'Ugh. Aye to all the above.' She poked him playfully in the arm. 'You are positively no fun, brother, but do not think I have forgotten what I just saw with my own eyes. You. Were. Smiling.'

'I think not. Perhaps you were imagining things.'

'I also have additional plans for the day. I am sorting through my chamber and deciding what shall stay and what I shall bring to my new home. Garrick will also be joining us for dinner this eve. Do not forget.' She dropped her voice to a whisper. 'How shall I introduce him to Mrs Gordon?'

He stopped short, and she paused alongside him. *Blast.* 'I'd forgotten that was tonight,' he said. 'Leave the introductions to me. I will speak with her before our dinner, so she is somewhat…prepared.'

'Shall I warn Garrick?' Brenna asked.

'And tell him what? That I have bought a bride?' He scoffed at her, his voice in a hushed whisper.

She pressed her lips together and shrugged. 'Maybe?'

He scrubbed a hand through his hair. 'He would think me mad. Tell him nothing. I shall explain to him when he arrives. I will think upon it until then.'

'He will understand, brother.'

'Brenna, how can he understand what even I cannot fathom?' He shook his head. 'I must go,' he grumbled. 'I must be prepared for when the elders arrive.'

'What is it you must speak with them about so early this morn?'

'Ironically, we were scheduled to discuss when I would be expected to take a wife.'

To his relief, she said nothing and let him walk away unscathed.

He stalked down the hallway, entered his study, and

closed the door loudly behind him. He rested his hands on his waist and paced the room. What exactly *would* he tell them?

I have bought a bride.

Nay.

I found a bride.

Nay.

I no longer need help in selecting a bride.

Maybe.

I have chosen a bride.

Better.

A knock on the door sounded.

'Aye,' he answered.

'They have arrived, my laird,' Mrs Stevens called. 'Shall I send them in?'

I have chosen a bride, it is.

'Aye. Send them in. You can leave the door open. Thank you, Mrs Stevens.'

Ewan reminded himself that he was laird, not them, as their heavy footfalls warned of their approach. He was leader of the clan, not they. Niven, the oldest and most difficult of them all, paused in the doorway, his dark, brooding countenance and large build like the weather itself. He was known to have the power to darken any room, and he was Ewan's father's oldest friend.

Niven nodded. 'My laird.'

Ewan nodded in kind. 'Good morn, Niven. Come in.'

Harris and Broden followed him, each offering a greeting and nod of respect before they settled into the chairs at the large table before them. How many times over the last century had terms been agreed to by his forefathers over this bruised wooden table? Ewan settled in last and pressed his palms flat to the wood, saying a prayer to be guided by patience and humility rather than arrogance, as he knew the men would test him. While he liked all three of them individually, together they created a trio of discord to be rivalled by even the most challenging of men. Ewan scarcely ever left one of their gatherings without either a megrim or a need to spar with his best soldier for a good hour to release the frustration and anger the men could stir within him.

Niven raised his coal-black eyes to Ewan's and set the tone of their gathering with a single phrase: 'Have you decided?'

While Ewan knew full well what he was enquiring about, he sought a delay in clarifying. 'Upon?' he asked.

Niven slammed the table with his open palm, and temper coloured his cheeks. 'You know full well what I am referring to. You need to select a bride *and* decide on what we shall do with the border we share with the MacGregors. Any further delays only put us at more risk. Times are growing increasingly uncertain in these parts with the uprisings against the king and so many alliances in question.'

'Aye. I do, and I have,' Ewan said. He narrowed his gaze at the veiled reference to their fractured alliance with the Robertsons caused by his disobedience. As if he needed any reminders of how his decision had negatively impacted the clan.

They all stared back at him, awaiting more information. 'And?' Harris chimed in.

'It will be announced.'

'When?' Broden asked, leaning closer. 'When I am dead, my laird?'

The other two men chuckled at that. Ewan avoided the bait and quoted one of his father's most irritating and effective replies. 'When I am ready. I am laird, after all.'

Their laughter dwindled to nothing, and they were back to the awkward silence of moments ago.

Ewan offered them a scrap. 'But I will approve the repairs to the stone wall and add soldiers along the northern border with the MacGregors. We'll not lose one more head of livestock to them, nor will we allow them to cross into our lands to get to the loch after all that has happened. They have taken advantage of our kindness long enough. If they don't like our new arrangement, then MacGregor can come to me straight away, and we can form some more permanent understanding. Go ahead and speak with your men about it this eve, and have the plan set in motion on the morrow.'

Niven sat back in his chair, studying him. 'And the marriage?'

'As I said, when I am ready, all will be revealed, as the terms of the arrangement are still being settled.' Ewan should have known that a scrap would not be enough for the old man. He wanted all when he wanted it. Not a moment sooner or later. It was one of the reasons why Niven and Ewan's father got on so well: they understood each other.

Niven pushed once more. 'By end of summer?'

Ewan didn't dignify the man's overt challenge to his authority by answering.

'Perhaps we should move on to our next order of business,' Broden offered, attempting to guide them along. No doubt he noted the precarious territory they were meandering into and hoped to pull them from it before the men came to verbal blows.

'What business is that?' Ewan enquired, not aware of any additional matters to be addressed this morn.

Harris glanced over to Broden and shrugged. 'Might as well tell him. Ye brought it up.'

'There's talk of whether we'll be overrun. Driven out by the British. Or absorbed by another clan. The villagers are nervous. They think we don't have enough weapons or men to protect us from either.'

Ewan leaned forward, resting his elbows on the table. 'Well, is there any truth to their concerns? Do we have enough arms and soldiers to fend off an attack, if needed?'

Harris and Broden looked down at the table. When neither answered, Niven said, 'Nay, my laird, we don't.'

'Why not? Where has the money usually spent for such a purpose gone to?' Ewan asked. 'I've seen the ledgers. There is money still set aside for just that purpose, and there has been for years.'

''Tis not enough, and we have but two blacksmiths who are skilled enough to make such goods. The rest have not the experience as they are not far enough along in their training.'

'Well, send out word, quietly, about taking on more skilled blacksmiths to forge for us. We must have weapons.'

'And the soldiers?'

He hesitated. 'I'll not take on men for hire. 'Tis too great a risk. They have little to no loyalty to anything or anyone other than coin.'

For once, the men nodded with him in agreement. 'An alliance, perhaps?' Broden offered.

'That is an idea. I will think upon our options over the coming week.'

'Do not think upon it too long, my laird. This is not the Scotland of your childhood. We are more vulnerable than we've been in quite some time. All of us who wear a kilt are. The British are pressing in on us. 'Tis only a matter of time before they attempt to take all of it from us.'

As the new laird, Ewan was as vulnerable as the clan, and the older men knew it. 'I'll expect an update on the rock wall and the men who will be on guard in the coming days,' Ewan stated as he stood, the signal that their meeting was at an end whether they had additional issues to discuss or not. He needed to escape what he knew would turn into a fruitless debate over the old and new Scotland if the conversation continued any longer.

The other two stood, with Niven being the last to rise, his face brimming with the words his lips no doubt wanted to say. But to Ewan's surprise, he nodded and followed the other men out without protest. Perhaps the meeting had gone better than Ewan had thought.

As Niven had almost cleared the door, he paused and faced Ewan. 'We both know your father would not have hesitated at the thought of seeking out an alliance to protect us. I hope you know what you're doing, my laird. Our livelihood and lives depend upon it.'

Before Ewan could censure the man for his disrespect and challenge to his authority, he was gone. Ewan slammed his fist on the table and cursed. Before he did anything rash, he pushed his way through the side door that led to the glen. He closed his eyes and sucked in one greedy breath after another and assured himself as he often did that he could be laird. He didn't have to be his father. He could be his own man. No matter how treacherous the path was.

And by all that was holy, he would be his own man without driving the clan into chaos and ruin.

'How did your meeting go, my laird?'

Ewan opened his eyes to find Catriona standing almost next to him without having heard her approach at all. 'Blazes. You could give a man a start with such a stealthy approach. If you'd meant to kill me, I'd be dead.' He scratched the back of his neck and shook his head.

The wind ruffled her skirts and the rogue locks of hair escaping her plait, and she smiled. 'Stealth is one of my many talents. You learn to be quiet to avoid being found or being hurt.' Her eyes dropped away from his gaze and settled on the glen and the loch far beyond them.

His stomach knotted at all that remained hidden within her words.

Before he could reply, Rufus gave a rowdy bark below and charged up the hill. Ewan smiled. His favourite wolfhound must have spied him and decided it was time for a game of fetch. The large, grey, wiry hound barrelled into him and would have knocked Ewan flat if he hadn't bent his leg to brace for impact. The hound was still as playful as a pup despite being almost four years of age. Ewan scratched him behind his left ear, and Rufus's left leg thumped on the ground.

'This is Rufus, and this is his favourite spot to be scratched,' Ewan said to Catriona, who stared down at the hound in awe.

'I've never had a dog before.'

'He won't bite. Just put your closed hand down for him to sniff.'

She did just that, and Rufus answered her interest in him with a slobbery kiss on her hand. She laughed and squatted beside him. Rufus abandoned Ewan and leaned heavily on Catriona before swiping a kiss to her cheek. Her laughter trilled out in the air, and Ewan stilled. She was even more beautiful when she was happy.

His chest tightened. Had he made a mistake in bringing her here? What if he made her miserable? What if he couldn't protect her? What if—

He caught sight of the scars across so many of her knuckles and chided himself.

You saved her. You can protect her. You might even make her happy. She might even make you happy.

That last thought cooled his blood. He didn't know if he feared that the most. Happiness never seemed to last in the Highlands. And wasn't not having it better than having it and losing it like he had with Emogene?

'Pence for your thoughts,' she called as Rufus landed another rogue kiss to her cheek.

He cleared his throat. 'Just my meeting.' He *had* been thinking upon it earlier, so perhaps it wasn't a complete lie.

Yes, it was. He tucked his hands in the pockets of his trews.

'Perhaps a walk in this fresh air will clear your head,' she offered as she stood. 'You can tell me about this place, you, and how I can help you, since I am to…stay awhile.' She paused, and he noticed she had failed to say she would be 'staying awhile' as his wife.

As he wondered upon the reasoning, she interrupted his thoughts and asked, 'Unless you have changed your mind?'

He faltered. Had he changed his mind? Was this doubt over his decision seeping in, and she was offering him a gentleman's way out of their hasty arrangement? He met her steady, unwavering gaze, her eyes amber pools flecked with gold and tiny hints of moss green. How he wished he had such certainty, such sense of self. No matter his answer, she appeared accepting of whatever came her way. Could she teach him such?

'Nay,' he answered. 'I have not changed my mind. Have you?'

Doubt flashed in her eyes before she answered. 'I have not, but I am acutely aware of what I lack here. Thrice now Betsy has chided me for doing her work. I find I do not know what to do with myself without chores and tasks to do every moment, and I have been here a day.'

She shrugged and laughed. Her ease was contagious, and he found himself relaxing as they walked along the meadow.

'Perhaps you can busy yourself with learning the clarsach,' he teased.

She shivered. 'You and I both know that will take some time, and it may drive your servants running from Glenhaven.'

'Then, you can help me in securing my position here. You said you are a keen judge of people. Perhaps you can help me get somewhere with my most challenging and peevish of clansmen: the elders. That was who I just met with.'

'I'd be happy to try on all accounts. It shall keep me from enduring Betsy's chiding.' Rufus nudged her leg with a stick he'd clearly fetched from somewhere. She took it from him, ruffled his ears, and threw the stick a vast distance down the glen.

'Or perhaps I shall enter you in the Tournament of Champions and have you put the best of the eligible lairds to shame come fall,' he said. 'That was quite some throw.'

'Oh?' She lifted her eyebrows and shrugged. 'Just gave it a toss, that's all.'

So she was strong, hardworking, and humble. He'd add them to the list of mysteries he was set on solving about her.

'Tell me of these leaders, these elders, although I would love to meet them. Seeing them in person would tell me a great deal. Perhaps they could come to dine?'

Ack. 'Dinner. Aye. A fine idea. I can invite them later in the week, but before I forget, Brenna's fiancé, Laird Garrick MacLean, is coming to dine with us this eve. Bren reminded me of it this morn. How shall I introduce you?'

She stopped, quirked her lips, and crossed her arms against her chest. 'Do you know him well?'

'Aye.'

'And you like him and trust him?'

'Aye. He is the best of men.'

'Then just tell him the truth. It shall be easiest until all is sorted.'

'You will not be…embarrassed by me speaking such truths to him about what happened in the market?'

'The truth has never bothered me. It is the lies I cannot keep up with,' she offered. 'I look forward to meeting him.' And with that, he watched her set off once more. Little unsettled her, while nearly everything unsettled him. How did one get to be so at ease with oneself and the world?

She paused. 'Coming?' she asked, turning to him.

'Aye,' he answered and jogged to catch up with her, distinctly aware of the irony of him being laird and certain of little while she had nothing and was quite certain of everything. There was something about her calm that settled him almost as much as her beauty unsettled him. It was an odd, heady mix to be sure, and he didn't quite know what to do with it.

Rufus charged off and then looped back around them as they travelled along the glen side by side. The tall green grass leaned to and fro in the breeze, and off in the distance, men worked in their fields while children played in front of their cottages with their mothers not far away. The scene was idyllic in every sense. He soaked it in. *This* was what he was working so hard for, wasn't it? Perhaps he needed to remember that the meetings and manoeuvrings were for a better and greater purpose far more important than him and his happiness. Thousands of people depended on him.

'Tell me of your meeting this morn with the clan leaders.'

Her enquiry caught him off guard. 'Do you truly wish to know?'

'Aye. How else can I help you with knowing who your greatest supporters and challengers are to your position?'

He couldn't remember a time when Mother had asked Father of anything regarding his meetings with the clan or the elders, but perhaps she asked in private, far away from the ears of their children. What did he have to lose? They were to be married, were they not? A partnership was born of trust, not secrets. Life had taught him that lesson well.

'They wished to speak with me about two main issues. The first was my marriage, for they are eager for me to claim a wife and secure my footing as the new laird within the Highlands by establishing an heir. The second was about the border with the MacGregors.'

She paused and smiled, plucking a small purple nettle from the grass. 'Well, hopefully you were able to solve at least one of them.' She tucked it behind her ear, a simple action that reminded him of a time when Emogene had done just that very thing before she'd left him heartbroken for another man, never to be seen again.

Her smile faltered. 'What is it? You've gone as pale as a ghost.'

'I must go,' he said hurriedly. 'I just remembered there is somewhere else I need to be.'

'I understand. Go on then. I'll be fine.' Her brow furrowed as she shielded the sun from her eyes with her hand.

His heart raced, and he turned to leave. He had to get away. He couldn't breathe. He couldn't see anything other than his history of losing the things he'd cared for and loved. Losing his mother, losing Emogene… Was he beginning to care for Catriona too? What if he loved her and lost her?

He couldn't and he wouldn't. It was as simple as that.

Chapter Ten

'That was odd,' Catriona muttered to Rufus. She knelt in the grass to pet his floppy ears and wiry hair.

One thing was for certain. She *knew* people, but Catriona couldn't understand this Laird Stewart at all. One moment he was sincere and attentive, and the next he flitted off like a startled thrush. 'Shall we walk on, you handsome devil?' she asked the pup, and he yipped in agreement. She climbed and then descended into the lower valley, tempted to walk into the village to meet more of the clan and knowing full well what a horrid idea that was. How exactly would she introduce herself?

My name is Mrs Catriona Gordon. The Laird bought me at the market to be his wife.

She cringed and retraced her steps to return to the castle. Veering a little further to the forest, she spied what appeared to be a small graveyard, even though there was no chapel in sight. She climbed the remaining distance and edged over to the headstones. Most were quite old and slightly overgrown with moss and a smattering of wildflowers, but there was one that seemed recent, with a wide area of disturbed ground. She knew whose it was before she even looked upon the carved letters.

His father.

And beside him was his wife, Ewan's mother.

Catriona ran her fingertips over the curling script of the chiselled stone. They had spared no expense in the monument to the laird and his wife. The headstones were of the finest polished slate. Under Laird Stewart's name was the family crest, and beneath Lady Stewart's name was a beautifully engraved cross and harp. Catriona smiled. It warmed her heart to know that Ewan had been loved by such a woman, even if their time together had been cut short. Now Catriona's fingers trailed along her necklace, and she tugged the worn silver locket from her bosom. It was the one thing she had from her past. Although she could not place from whence she'd got it, she'd always had it, and it gave her great comfort each time she touched it. The design on the locket was worn away in some places from her own touch over the years. She'd used it as a worry stone and comfort when she had been frightened, alone, or desperate. She had felt that way quite often over the years since she'd been found along the shoreline by Nettie, with no memory of who she was or where she was from. She'd protected the necklace with her life and felt as connected to it as the air in the sky and the soil beneath her feet.

She tucked it back in her bodice and lifted her skirts as she began the walk back to the castle. Rufus had long since abandoned her on her journey. Far too many furry temptations abounded. Betsy waved to her as Catriona approached, and the young lass smiled until she spied the bottom of her dress. Following her gaze, Catriona looked down. Her beautiful dress was stained all along the hemline from her exploits through the meadow, as were her walking boots.

She cringed. 'I will help you set them to rights,' Catriona offered. 'I should have been more careful. I'm not used to having to worry upon ruining my clothes. There wasn't much to ruin in the past.' Her cheeks warmed.

'No harm done,' Betsy replied. 'I have mended far worse than this. Let us get ye back inside and changed before the laird sees ye.'

Catriona stiffened. 'Why? Will he be angry?'

The man hadn't seemed the type to be concerned with such trifles, but she didn't know him. Not really.

Betsy paused, studying her. 'Nay. I did not mean to alarm ye. He is a good man and not prone to fits of temper like his father was.'

Catriona still didn't move. 'You are sure? I don't wish you to be in trouble either.'

Betsy grasped her forearm. 'Nay,' she assured her. 'There is no cause for alarm. Let us get ye inside and changed.'

Catriona nodded and followed the maid, her heart still thrumming in her chest. It would be hard to unlearn the fear that could spike within her at the slightest hint of displeasing whatever authority loomed over her. It mattered not if it was an employer or a husband. The fear of being hit or chided as she had been in the past brought out the wee lass in her, and once she was out, it was quite hard to settle her down.

Pulling in a breath, she reminded herself that she was safe with a man who seemed kind and in a place that could offer her more than she had ever dreamed possible. While not free, she would have more freedoms than before and experience new things each day. Chores would not fill all her waking hours. The exploration of interests would mark her days. She might even discover other facets of herself never allowed to emerge. She could be one of the butterflies she was always so intrigued by and emerge from a cocoon into something spectacular.

Her boot sank into a glob of mud.

Or things might be the same.

But one thing was for certain. She'd never find out if she didn't go inside and change.

She'd also never know the truth about the laird's past if she didn't enquire. She fell into stride next to Betsy as they climbed the final hill to the castle door.

'Has the laird been married before?' Catriona asked.

Betsy's pace hitched for a mere moment, and then she continued on. 'Nay, my lady.'

She quirked her lips. He sure acted like a man spurned. 'A broken engagement, perhaps?'

Betsy walked a step closer and opened the door. 'Not here,' she whispered. 'May I take your shoes?' she asked in a normal voice as a footman passed. Catriona bent down to assist her in removing them.

The servant turned the corner. 'Is it a secret?' she asked.

The worry in the young maid's eyes sent Catriona's heart aflutter. The lass shook her head. Catriona's heart dropped. Had something scandalous happened? Was the laird cruel after all?

Betsy grabbed Catriona's shoes and continued. Catriona followed her in her stocking feet. By the time they reached her chamber and sealed the door shut behind them, Catriona had crafted a story in her mind of Laird Stewart as a murderer and a cheat.

'And?' Catriona asked.

'Let us get ye out of this first,' Betsy began to undo the column of buttons down Catriona's back.

'Betsy, by all that is holy, you must tell me. I need know the man I am to marry before I commit to him.'

Betsy froze. 'Are ye not already married, Mrs Gordon?'

Catriona cringed. *Blast.* Silence ticked by, and then she sighed. 'You must tell no one, you promise me?' she pleaded and faced her maid.

Betsy nodded with her hands still mid-air. 'Aye.'

'The laird purchased me at the Grassmarket. My husband sold me to him.'

'What?' she asked. 'A man cannot sell or buy a wife. 'Tis not legal,' she argued, crossing her arms against her chest. She seemed full of outrage and disbelief, much like Catriona had felt.

'That is what we are trying to find out. Until then, I will remain here.' She left out the part about them marrying in hopes Betsy might conveniently forget that piece of information.

The maid narrowed her eyes at her. 'But ye just said, "But I need to know the man I am to marry *before* I commit to him." One cannot marry a man if ye are already married…can ye?'

'Ugh…' Catriona groaned and hid her face in her hands. 'Nay. One cannot marry again if one is still married, but we do not know if this transaction in the marketplace was even legal. I had planned to run last night to free myself and him from this conundrum, but he asked me to stay. Proposed to me, even. I need to know why. Why would a laird such as him propose to me? It makes little sense. He is handsome, young, and seems quite normal by all accounts. Don't you agree?'

Betsy seemed struck dumb and said nothing for a few moments. She then closed her gaping mouth and sputtered out a reply. 'I agree. It makes no sense to me, my lady. The fathers have been all but parading their daughters by him, and the laird has been tasked with accepting one of them by the end of the month. He has many options other than…'

Thank goodness the lass stopped short of adding *you* on the end of the sentence, to spare Catriona some of her pride.

'So that is why I must know what has happened to him that would make him choose me: a woman he does not know, with no family, money, or title. What would make him do such?'

'Loss.'

Her answer was simple and landed heavily on Catriona's heart.

'Loss? What kind of loss? His mother? He told me of that.'

Betsy returned to unbuttoning Catriona's dress and

.continued. 'It all happened about six years ago when I was a teen and living with my parents in the village. The laird was engaged to the most beautiful lass in the clan: Emogene.'

Catriona held her breath.

'But the engagement came at a great cost. Ewan was supposed to marry Laird Robertson's daughter. When Ewan went against the arrangement and his father's orders by becoming engaged to Emogene, it fractured the alliance between our two clans, and Ewan was close to blows with his father. It brought great shame upon him, the family, and the clan. Then, weeks before Ewan and Emogene were set to marry, she ran off and married a Sutherland who had greater wealth and power.'

Catriona gasped. 'So he was left with no wife and with the knowledge that he had harmed his clan's future?'

'Aye. It was horrible.'

'What happened to Ewan?' Catriona's chest ached.

'When he realised what she'd done, he didn't speak for days, and then disappeared for several weeks. When he returned, he never spoke of her again and raged at anyone who dared say her name. She became a ghost after that. Many say so did he.'

'He doesn't seem a ghost now.'

She shrugged. 'Perhaps not, but is he really living either? I've heard the stories of him swearing off love and attachments.'

The lass's words hit Catriona like an arrow hitting its mark. 'Aye. That is true. It is one of the reasons he said we'd make such a fine match.'

'Oh?' Betsy asked. 'Why is that?'

'Because he does not know me or care for me at all. And he wishes to keep it that way.'

Chapter Eleven

'Mrs Gordon is quite lovely and an unexpected surprise this eve,' Garrick offered as he approached Ewan, who stood near the mantel of the large, empty fireplace off the dining room.

Ewan sipped from his tankard, uncertain.

Garrick nodded towards the two women. 'Even Bren seems taken with her, which is quite a feat, as you well know.' His friend chuckled, as Bren was known to be devilishly hard on other women and took on new female friends like oil took on water, which was rarely.

'Aye,' Ewan dared. The two ladies sat on the settee chatting, which was really Bren rattling on about her wedding and Catriona listening attentively.

'Care to tell me what the devil is going on?'

It was Ewan's turn to laugh. His friend's directness was as sharp as a dirk, but well intended. The man wasn't capable of cruelty, just as Ewan seemed incapable of certainty. He risked taking Catriona's advice and telling him the truth.

'The day before yesterday, when I took Bren into

Edinburgh for a dress fitting and to visit her favourite milliner, I bought Mrs Gordon in the Grassmarket.'

Garrick stared at him.

'It is a fine situation that leaves you speechless, Mac-Lean.'

Garrick shook his head and stuttered out a reply. 'Sorry, did you say *bought*?'

His face heated. 'It was the better of two horrid options.' He shifted on his feet and gestured for Garrick to follow him outside. His friend sent a glance back in the ladies' direction and then followed him out of doors.

'I was wandering about the market looking upon the wares when I heard a man calling out that he was selling his wife. There were even handing out broadsides with the announcement, if you can believe it.'

'Just when I thought I'd heard all things,' Garrick replied, pinching the bridge of his nose.

'At first, I thought it a farce, but then when I walked through the crowd and saw her there—' his throat tightened '—bound in a harness like some bloody animal, I couldn't think straight. And then, when Dallan Mac-Gregor chimed in to buy her for even less than her arse of a husband was offering, I just reacted. I offered to buy her for the full price, to save her. All I could think of was… Moira.'

'Ewan,' Garrick began, his eyes softening in sympathy, 'you cannot blame yourself.'

'Actually, I can,' he answered. 'If I'd paid more attention and been less distracted by my own affairs, I might have noticed what was happening to her. But since I didn't, and because I cannot unwind the past, when I saw Mrs Gordon in such distress and knowing worse could happen to her if MacGregor got a hold of her, I couldn't let it be. I gave her husband a guinea and hustled her out of there before the sot could change his mind.'

'You bought her for a guinea?' Garrick asked in disbelief.

'Aye. I'd like to think I merely freed her for a guinea. And it seemed her husband, Mr Gordon, would have taken less.'

'Lord above,' Garrick murmured.

'Aye.'

'And your plan now?' Garrick asked before taking a drink from his cup.

'I sent word to my solicitor to enquire over whether any of it was legal, as the broadside stated that by buying her she would instantly become my wife, which I cannot imagine to be true. Receiving the answer will take time. She will stay here until that is sorted.' He hesitated.

'And?'

'And I asked her to marry me when we know for certain that she is free of Mr Gordon.'

Garrick coughed, almost spitting out his wine. 'What?'

'You heard me. I mean to take her as my wife.' An unspoken challenge rested in the sharp edge of his voice even though it wasn't what he intended.

Garrick held up his hands. 'She is beautiful and quite charming, but you do not *know* her. You do not even know if what you did was legal or if she can even divorce this Mr Gordon.' He stepped closer and dropped his voice. 'And selecting a wife outside of the clan is sure to cause you more harm than good.'

Ewan dragged a palm down his face. 'Of course. I *know* that,' he replied, 'but I also know I'll make enemies with any bride I choose within the clan. Even now they jostle for power, biding their time while hoping for my failure.' He drank the last of his tankard. 'What would you do?'

Garrick chuckled. 'You mean if I still had a clan to rule?'

Deuces. Ewan cringed. 'You know that isn't what I meant. And you and I both know you will have your clan assembled once more and Westmoreland returned to rights. It will merely take time and patience.'

Garrick smiled good-naturedly. 'Aye. I do know. And I have plenty of both these days. But why do you not take your own advice and be patient with yourself as you get settled in as the new laird? You cannot expect it to fall into place in only a few months.'

'Time is not something I can afford to waste. All the Highland lairds as well as the leaders within our clan are watching my every move, and the MacGregors continue to breach our borders and steal from our herds. The elders complain that I do not make decisions fast enough, and I worry that I will make them too quickly and make a costly misstep. Why did no one tell me being a laird is an impossible task? No one is ever happy.'

'Were you expecting to be adored?' Garrick asked.

'Aye.' Ewan chuckled. 'I was hoping to be.'

'So, now that you really know what it is like to be laird, what is your plan?' Garrick asked. 'You cannot mean to take this woman to be your wife when you do not know her. She could be a criminal for all you know.'

'A criminal?' Ewan asked, frowning at his friend and gesturing towards Catriona, who was cooing to Rufus and ruffling the hound's ears. The woman had convinced him to let the dog in after they dined. 'Perhaps a touch persuasive, but that is no crime.'

Garrick's gaze followed Ewan's to the ladies.

'You think that woman is a mastermind trying to overthrow the clan with subterfuge and intrigue? Is her crime spoiling my hound?'

Garrick conceded. 'Perhaps not, but what do you know of her? You don't even know if she will be *able* to marry you legally. All I'm suggesting is not to rush into a betrothal. Why don't you at least have a trial of time together before either of you commits to each other for the rest of your lives? Those seem the fairest terms for both of you, especially if her past marriage has been as difficult as it appears.'

Hmm... 'Like a trial marriage?' His gaze skimmed over Catriona's petite features as her head tilted back with laughter at something Brenna had said.

'Of sorts.'

Ewan paused. His friend might very well be onto a fine suggestion. 'That's not the most ridiculous idea I've ever heard. Perhaps we could see how it goes, and if I don't find that I wish to become her husband and she my wife, say in a fortnight's time or until we hear back from the solicitor, we will dissolve our agreement and be free of one another.'

'And if you do decide you want her to be your wife?' Garrick asked with a smirk.

'Then perhaps I will become a married man before you are, Garrick MacLean.'

'Remember, she would have to choose you willingly as well.'

'In that case, you may well beat me to the altar after all.'

Chapter Twelve

Catriona hummed as she walked down the hallway to her chambers, her belly rather full of another lovely dinner. She glanced behind and, noting the hallway was empty, she tugged off her slippers and stockings. When her bare feet touched the cool, clean floor, she sighed, rolling the balls of her feet and her toes. She felt so carefree and happy, just like that girl on the beach laughing with the sun warming her face and the sand between her toes.

She twirled once and then twice down the hallway, her skirts flying freely and lifting in the air, exposing her ankles. She chuckled aloud and hummed one of her favourite tunes as if she were dancing in a ball with a handsome laird.

'Mrs Gordon?'

Blazes.

She stumbled to a stop and turned, hiding her shoes and stockings behind her back. 'Aye, my laird?' She blew an errant lock of hair from her eyes. Blasted useless hairpins.

Ewan cleared his throat, his gaze wandering over her face and then drifting down to her bare feet. She flushed. He wasn't immediately able to continue, his gaze lingering on her toes so long that she looked down to ensure her feet hadn't turned into flippers.

'My laird?' she asked again, feeling awkward and self-conscious.

He shifted on his feet, her words yanking him back from wherever he'd gone. 'I wish to have a word with you about what we discussed last night. Discuss some new terms of our arrangement. Do you have a moment?'

Her pulse thrummed. There was something in the way he said the words that made worry skitter along her spine. He'd changed his mind about something. Perhaps it was about her? Had his friend, Laird MacLean, told him how unreasonable and ridiculous it was to marry her? Did he finally see the fault in such a scheme? Would he cast her out this eve? Despite having wished to escape the night before, worry about doing just that bubbled up in her now.

Why?

If he offered her freedom, wasn't that exactly what she had wanted? Why would she not wish to leave now? Before she could answer that, she felt herself nodding her head as if she were no longer attached to or controlling her body. Instinct was setting in, a survival tool she had harnessed well over the years. While part of her was present, the other part was scheming and seeking out a way to escape. It was a facet of her she couldn't turn off, not yet at least.

'Would you like to put your shoes back on? I thought

we'd step outside since the weather is so fine this eve and you enjoy the stars.'

'Or you could take your shoes off as well, my laird? It is such fine weather, as you have just stated.' Her voice held defiance. What had come over her? The words had tumbled from her mouth unbidden, as if they had escaped of their own free will. She was in no position to defy him about anything, yet here she was, doing just that. Disbelief registered in his eyes.

When his lip quirked up and his rogue dimple winked at her in answer, she almost giggled aloud. 'Is that a challenge, Mrs Gordon?'

She pressed her lips together to hold back her laughter once more. 'Aye, my laird, it is. What say you?' She tilted her head, brought her shoes from behind her back and clacked the heels together.

He chuffed off one boot, then another, followed by his own stockings. The sight of his muscular calves and large bare feet sent a thrill of attraction through her. He was such a handsome creature. The light sparkled off his eyes as he lifted his boots and clacked the heels together in answer. 'I say you have a deal, Mrs Gordon.'

She couldn't have been more enthralled by a man as she was in that very moment. She had cast a test, and he'd answered in kind. Her pulse increased, and she smiled.

'Care to expand it to a wager?' he asked.

She stepped closer, and then dared another step, her gaze slipping down to his glorious legs and feet once more. 'Aye. First one to the grass gets a wish from the other.'

'You're on,' he answered. 'I'll even give you a head start.'

'I shan't need it, my laird,' she chided, but then darted off.

He counted to five and gave chase. The man was fleet of foot and quickly gained on her as they rushed along the main corridor. She banked right and then a final left. She could see the doors to the outside, just as she could hear the slapping of the soles of his bare feet along the floor behind her as they passed the last lit torch before the outdoors. As she slowed to reach the handle and open the door, he reached her, and together they flew out through the doors at the same time. Unable to slow her speed, she tumbled down part of the hill. She skidded to a stop on her backside and laughed aloud with glee. A laugh so pure and full that her stomach ached. She had not laughed so hard in ages.

Ewan slid down the grass and stopped next to her, a smile on his face. 'Are you harmed?' he asked, out of breath. He brushed the hair from her eyes, and his fingertips lingered along her cheek. His expression held the slightest uncertainty, a veiled concern for her safety.

She grasped his hand and squeezed. 'I am fine. However, Betsy may become apoplectic when she sees I have stained yet another lovely gown today.' She cringed.

''Tis no matter,' he answered, sitting down beside her in the cool, lush grass.

She flopped back into the lawn, revelling in the cool, crisp smell of the field, the dark sky with its perfect stars, and feeling so free. Freer than she had ever felt. While she knew she was still bound to another man, the realisation of it did not sting her, for this man made her *feel* free.

Ewan stared down at her in silence, his gaze holding an answer and a question all at once, which seemed to be the way of him.

'What?' she asked.

'You are definitely not the woman I expected when I first saw you.'

'Did you even see me?' she challenged.

He shook his head. 'Not really. Nay. I didn't. I couldn't see anything. I just reacted.'

'Why?' she countered, wanting to know the truth. 'Why risk getting involved? You saw how many men walked by and did nothing. Why did you step in as you did?' She propped herself up on her elbow. She'd wanted to know the answer for days.

He hesitated. His eyes beat back and forth, searching hers, but for what? Acceptance? The truth? Certainty?

'Because of what happened to my eldest sister, Moira,' he said. He looked away and stared back up at the sky. 'Her first husband was cruel. He hurt her...' He paused, a muscle flexing in his jaw. 'And we did not know what was happening, how he abused her, until he was dead. I've always wished I'd paid more attention, known what was happening, so I could have stopped it as a brother should. I promised myself that if I ever saw anything like that occur again, I would step in.'

He faced her then, studying her, assessing her response.

'I am so very sorry that happened to her. Is she cared for now?' she asked, her throat tight.

He smiled. 'Aye. She is remarried to a kind, good man who cares for her and protects her and their children.' His smile deepened. 'You would like one another; I am sure of it.'

'I'm sure we would.'

His brow creased. 'May I ask… How did you end up with him, your husband, I mean?'

She cleared her throat and released a breath preparing to tell him of her past, since he had just shared about his sister.

'Well, Nettie cared for me for several years after she found me along the shore, but she died when I was thirteen, and I had no one to care for me. A family took me in on Lismore, and at first, all was well. I helped care for their children, did chores, and I thought about how lucky I was to find another kind family to care for me.' She paused. 'But then one night, the father had far too much to drink and lost his temper, hitting his wife and then one of his children. After that, I used to bait him when he was angry, so that if he was to lash anyone, than it would be me rather than them. I did not want to see the children hurt. They were so small.'

He reached out and took her hand, squeezing it briefly before letting go. 'I am so sorry, Catriona. That was an incredibly brave thing to do, especially for a young girl.'

She shrugged. 'Like you, I did not think about it, but merely reacted. When I told a neighbour what was happening, she helped to secure me a position with a wealthy family, the Chisholms, in a neighbouring village. I worked as a servant, and there I learned to read and write. Although I often sent back money to that family to help them, I always worried about what was happening there. The neighbour promised to look after them, but… And one day I met Thomas at the market while I was picking up the Chisholm children's new clothes. I thought he was my chance to have a family and be happy, but I was wrong.'

'I am glad you are here now,' he replied.

'I am grateful that you brought me here.' And she was. Attraction was buzzing through her.

'What do I get as my prize, since I did win our foot race?' She grinned at him.

He flopped back in the grass. 'It was a tie.'

'How on earth could that possibly be a tie, when I touched the doorknob first?'

He propped himself back up on his elbow to answer. 'Because without me turning the handle and pushing it open, we would have slammed into the door stacked upon each other in a quite unceremonious way.'

She blushed at the thought of how intimate such a scene might have been. A small part of her wished just that very thing had happened, and she chided herself. *Fool.* She needed to focus on the purpose of their talk: to discuss the terms of their agreement. Not to get caught up in a fairy tale of falling in love with a laird, especially when love was never to be part of their arrangement, if indeed there was still one. Perhaps his whole point of speaking with her was to cast aside their agreement all together?

He brushed aside his hair from his face, the subtle

action making her wish it was she who'd had such a familiar touch along his forehead.

Blazes. Get hold of yourself, Catriona.

She needed to stop looking upon him. Letting herself fall back in the grass, she sighed and closed her eyes. That was much better.

'Catriona?' he asked, leaning over her, his handsome face even closer than before, his brow stitched with concern. 'Are you unwell?'

She sucked in a breath. 'Nay. I am fine. Merely looking upon the stars, which you are now blocking.'

His face slipped back into its familiar mask, and he moved, settling into the grass beside her.

She cringed. She hadn't meant to sound so harsh, but she needed to get him away from her somehow. Her fingers itched to touch him, which was altogether ridiculous. She hardly knew him.

Deuces.

Ewan frowned, interlocking his fingers behind his head to prop it up. He could not remember when he'd last lain in the grass like this and felt so free and alive. And with a woman as beautiful and glorious as Catriona? *Never.*

He could not imagine a woman who would be so at ease lying in a field at night next to an unfamiliar man. And he'd mucked it up. Badly. That look on her face spoke far more than her words ever could.

What had he done to cause such a shift in her mood?

Perhaps he'd moved too close or asked too many prying questions. He would need to be far more careful in the future if he intended to make her his bride, which he did. The more unplanned moments he spent with her, the more he craved to know every part of her. When he'd heard her laugh earlier, it felt like air spilling into his lungs and as if the ground was shaking under his feet. A sickness roiled through his stomach, warning him of the danger ahead.

Ack. He had to be careful.

This was a truly ridiculous feeling that he had to keep at bay. He was treading in a field of thistles barefoot and hoping not to get barbed.

Nay. He would not fall in love with her; it was a ruin he had scarce survived once with Emogene, and he had promised himself never to swim into such deadly waters again. Loving and losing Emogene had broken him, and he wasn't sure if he'd ever been put together rightly since then. His heart was jagged edges and pock marks.

But it didn't mean that he couldn't enjoy Catriona's company. He could care for her as any good man would care for a wife. Without giving over his heart, he could revel in the long dormant passion and desire that she had awakened in him. But first, he needed to seal their new terms. For as much as he did believe she was right for him, he needed to be sure. And he also wanted her to have the option to choose him as well. This trial marriage, if one could call it that, would protect them both, and from what he had just learned about her past, the woman deserved protecting.

Being a laird's wife was about as precarious as being the laird himself. Not only would she have to manage him and all his foibles, but also the ever-shifting political ground beneath their feet, all while raising their children. The woman also deserved to make the choice for herself, a far greater gift than his sisters had ever had when Father had secured their dreadful first matches. Both had been disastrous, with his sisters scarcely surviving with their lives. Ewan wanted his marriage to benefit him and his bride.

'Shall we talk of your new terms, my laird?' she asked, her words snatching him back from his own thoughts and to the matter at hand. Despite being beside him, she sounded far away, her voice small and brittle, as if she stood in the valley below, calling up to the hillside.

'Aye. Laird MacLean had a great suggestion that I think will benefit us both.'

'Oh? I am surprised he did not disapprove entirely of our plan.' A touch of mirth entered her voice, and he smiled.

'Nay. Garrick is a good and thoughtful man with the sound, steady reason of a soldier seasoned by battle and loss.'

'Hmm. That makes sense to me now. There is loss in his eyes when he thinks no one is watching.'

Catriona's words cut Ewan to the quick, and he held his breath for a beat, gathering himself before answering. '*That* is the type of awareness that cannot be taught. It is such that I wish for you to teach me as my wife.'

'Do you not have men who advise you? Men you trust who serve you and your best interests first and foremost?' She propped up on her elbow once more, and he dared to do the same.

Did he?

'I have men who were loyal to my father who now serve me, but I do not believe that is the same.'

'Then why have you not pulled men you trust into your ranks and replaced the others? You are laird. You can do anything you wish, can you not?' Her brow furrowed. She studied him and shrugged. 'Or perhaps it is not so simple?'

'Aye. It is and isn't.' He plucked a wildflower from the grass and handed it to her. The bloom was closed for the eve but would open full in the morn. Just as he hoped she would open up to him over time.

She chuckled. 'You sound like a laird, but what do *you*, Ewan Stewart, mean by such an answer?'

What did he mean?

His heart beat feverishly in his chest. *This* was what he didn't want her to know: his weakness. He didn't know how to be laird. He didn't even know how to express his own opinion. For so long he'd been under the thumb of his father. How could he learn to trust his own mind, especially when he'd made such bad decisions before?

'Ewan?'

'I do not wish to change too much too quickly. Especially when there is such discord in the ranks after Father's passing.'

'Discord?' she asked. 'They cannot challenge you, for you are the son of the laird. Why would there be discord?'

'Aye. Only some of the conflict comes from my rule. Edinburgh has not been touched by the hand of the

British in the unrest as we have been in the Highlands. Clans have been absorbed and disappeared. Driven from their homes. Murdered for their lands. I must protect us from being absorbed by more powerful clans and attempt to keep my people happy. What I wish is not always part of that.'

'I suppose that makes sense.' She studied him, her eyes glinting in the moonlight. Her face as soft, smooth, and brilliant as the flower she held and twirled in her fingers.

He cleared his throat. It was now or never. 'So, my revised proposal would be that we allow each other a fortnight or until we hear from the solicitor, whichever comes first, to get to know each other and see if a marriage between us could suit us or not. During that time, you could see how comfortable you felt about the idea of being my wife. You could observe my duties and what it would mean for you to be the wife of a laird. You could also observe and report back to me your thoughts on the men and women of the clan and whom you think I should bring into my inner circle to keep our clan safe, prosperous, and thriving with me at the helm of it. You could teach me how to know and understand the motives, happiness, and dissatisfaction of those around me better than I do now. Many of them are as well-versed in deception as you are in observation and knowing people.'

'And you wish to be as well?'

'Nay. Not in being deceptive, but in being able to recognise it in others.'

'That is your new term?'

'Nay, just part of it. The other is that if we decide we do not wish to become husband and wife, then we will part and move on with our own lives without any additional explanation needed.'

Her eyes widened. 'And if I decided to leave? You would not be angry with me?' Doubt rested in her eyes as if she herself did not believe the words he said.

He nodded. 'I will send you on to the destination of your choice in my own carriage with your allowance as well as any personal items you wish to keep from your stay. You could start your own life, and I would not stop you.'

There was a small hitch in his voice, which surprised him, but he cleared his throat and continued. 'By then, we should also know if your marriage to Mr Gordon or my…agreement with him in purchasing you as a wife is legally binding or not.'

'And what shall you tell everyone, my laird? Surely it would seem odd to have a woman here for such an extended stay without reason?'

She made a solid point. 'Perhaps you are a cousin?' he said. 'Or a friend of an acquaintance?'

'A dead one, I hope. Otherwise, how will I answer all their questions about why I'm unchaperoned?'

'Perhaps I could enlist Laird MacLean to claim you as a distant cousin, since he is in on our ruse anyway.'

She tilted her head back and forth, seeming to ponder such a possibility. 'That could work. Do you think he would agree to it?'

'Aye. I think he would. He is to be my brother-in-law,

after all. We will be keeping each other's secrets from here on out for the rest of our lives.'

'But do you think he will keep mine, even if I choose to leave?'

The idea of her leaving sent an odd current of alarm through his limbs, but he ignored it. 'As I said before, you cannot find a better man. He would keep your secret to protect your honour and your future.'

'Then, I believe, Laird Stewart, we have a renewed agreement.' She sat up and narrowed her gaze at him. 'But there are still the terms of the wager I won earlier to be settled.'

He laughed and sat up as well. 'Terms?'

'You said the winner could have one thing they wished.'

'And here I thought we had agreed that we had both won.'

'I still claim victory. Do you call me a liar? Shall this be our first disagreement as pretend husband and wife?' She crossed her arms against her chest and gave him a playful glare of disapproval.

'Perhaps. For I claim we could never have reached the outside without me helping you open the door.'

She held his gaze undeterred. Her fire and resolve to claim her prize only fanned the flames of his budding interest and attraction to her. 'Then we may be at an impasse, my laird.'

'May I suggest a truce?' he said. 'What if we both claim victory and both are allowed a prize? Would that suit you?'

'While I would prefer to claim the victory as my own,

I could be persuaded to allow a joint victory this one time. What is it you wish to claim, my laird?'

You.

The answer hit him hot and full in his gut. The desire for her seared through him as if he had touched a blacksmith's iron without a glove. He swallowed that answer away, but not before his gaze fell and lingered upon her lips.

Her eyes widened, but she recovered from her alarm, squaring her shoulders and schooling her features. She was no fool as to what he wanted, so he decided not to attempt to disguise it. He risked the truth—well, at least part of it. 'A kiss,' he stated.

She shifted on the grass and nodded. 'All right, then.'

Her ready agreement shocked him, but he recovered. 'And yours? What is it you require of me for your prize?'

'A secret.'

He watched her, awaiting more.

'Tell me of the woman who broke your heart. Tell me of Emogene.' Her eyes held his, unflinching and powerful in their demand.

He clenched his fists by his sides. How dare she ask something so impossible, so personal, and so infuriating?

'What you ask I cannot give you.' He stood and brushed off his trews. 'I shall take my leave.' He began to walk away, but she called to him.

'And that, my laird, is what shall cost you in the end. You cannot allow anyone to know your weaknesses.'

'Oh? Does it not work both ways, Mrs Gordon? For you have also just shown me yours.'

* * *

'What?' she asked, but he continued walking without answering. She stood and rushed after him, a bud of anger tightening in her chest. 'I have revealed nothing to you. I merely challenged your past.'

He whipped around, his figure towering over her. His eyes were heated and wild in a way she had never seen, and his hair ruffled in the breeze. 'Nay. You have done far more than that. You have taken your finger and stuck it into an open wound on purpose. Why?' He took a step, and even though they weren't touching, she could feel the heat of his body. 'Because you don't wish for me to kiss you?'

She fought the urge to take one more step and set her hands upon his chest, curious to feel what was sure to be rippling muscle beneath. For as much as she was loath to admit it, she feared his touch. Not that he might hurt her, but that she might like it far too much. 'Aye,' she answered in reply.

'Why?' he asked. 'You came willingly with me out of doors in the night, and I have done nothing to make you fear me. I am not the sort of man to take advantage. If I was, I would have already. You insult me by suggesting as much, especially after all I have confessed to you about my sister.' Hurt registered in his features, which intrigued her. It was as if being feared as a danger to women was more of an insult than being inept as laird.

'Because I do not trust myself,' she answered, taking another step and resting her palm against his chest, savouring the warmth beneath his thin tunic.

He sucked in a breath. 'Do you tease me, Mrs Gordon? I fear I do not understand you. You do not wish for me to kiss you because you do not trust yourself, not because you fear me?'

'Aye. That is exactly why.'

'Then perhaps you should take your hand off my chest and stop looking at me that way. Otherwise, I *will* have to kiss you.'

'Then maybe you should.'

'Which is more reason why I shouldn't, for I cannot fulfil my end of the bargain by answering your enquiry, can I? And the last thing I wish is to appear an untrustworthy mate,' he quipped, the harsh snap to his words reflective of his anger. He stepped back, and her hand fell away. 'Until tomorrow, Mrs Gordon.'

He turned and left her in the field, his dark form disappearing into the backdrop of the sky. What she had hoped might give her an upper hand in their arrangement had just set her back twofold. For now, she did not know if he could ever get over his hurt regarding Emogene. Also, he knew she found him attractive. He could use both as a weapon to bring her to her knees.

She smiled. But perhaps so could she.

Chapter Thirteen

The next morning, Catriona found herself practicing the clarsach with little success. Her irritation over her current failings with the instrument and frustrations from her encounter the night before with Ewan threatened to drive her mad. The man seemed determined to avoid her this morn, having broken his fast well before dawn, according to Mrs Stevens. Brenna had yet to rise, so Catriona had eaten alone. The day was spinning into one irritation after another. She plucked another series of strings and cringed. Perhaps she should just leave the estate and the laird while she could before the two weeks were out. She wasn't meant to be idle. Nettie had taught her at a young age how the mundane routine of physical labour and chores could be used to ease worry from her body. Catriona's body and mind were used to such work through her servitude at the Chisholms' home and years of marriage. Despite how she had long wished to have time to explore other interests, now she wasn't sure, especially with so much restless energy churning through her body. A handful of days into her so called new life and 'freedom', and she was almost bored to tears.

'Mrs Gordon, the laird has need of ye,' Betsy called from the doorway of the salon as if she were an angel sent from the heavens to spare Catriona from her struggles.

And the idea of Ewan summoning her in any way made Catriona smile. Perhaps he was not as angry with her after their encounter last night as she had feared. At least, she hoped that was the reason for such a request. She'd find out soon enough, wouldn't she?

'Thank you, Betsy. You have saved me from further frustration.' Catriona rose and followed the maid through the castle. When they passed the laird's study and continued down another corridor unknown to her, uncertainty surfaced. 'Where am I meeting the laird?' Catriona whispered. 'I have never been this way before. What is down here?'

When Betsy said nothing but quickened her pace, Catriona picked up her skirts and hustled up to the maid's side. 'Where are we going?' she whispered to the lass.

Betsy glanced over to her. 'The laird bade me bring ye out this side of the castle. He did not say why.'

'And as the maid, you did not ask.'

'Aye. It is never my business to question his orders, my lady.'

Betsy stopped at the last door on the hallway. 'He said ye were to leave through this door and follow the tunnel to the end, and that I was not to accompany ye.'

'Did you say a tunnel was connected to the castle?'

'Aye. On this one portion. Built as an escape when needed.'

Was it needed today? And if so, why? Questions spooled in her mind, but she dared not ask. No doubt, the more questions the young maid answered, the more questions Catriona would have.

'Thank you, Betsy. I will see you later this afternoon to dress for dinner.'

She hoped.

'Aye. Enjoy your journey.'

Journey?

Before Catriona could gather some clarification on what 'journey' Betsy referenced, the maid curtseyed and left Catriona in the corridor. There were no windows near the doorway, so she wasn't sure exactly where she was or where this supposed tunnel would lead. Unease sidled up to her as she nudged the door open a sliver. But what choice did she have? She had no idea where she was, and Betsy was gone.

Blast.

She pushed the door completely open. It was a tunnel as promised and a dark one at that. If not for the wall torches burning brightly at regular intervals, she would not have been able to travel more than a step at a time for fear of tripping over her own feet. The door closed behind her, and she grabbed for the handle. She tugged, but it didn't budge.

Drat.

Forward it was, then. It was lucky she wasn't scared of the dark or confined spaces. Otherwise, she might have screamed. She started her journey, slowly and with caution. Despite being so hidden, the tunnel appeared carved from rock or part of a mountain. It was also quite wide. Two people could walk side by side as they travelled. Perhaps Ewan hadn't sent her to an early demise after all. Knowing that helped her relax. She studied the tunnel as she walked, running her hand down the cool, hard walls, carved with care and worn from use. The soles of her boots gripped the sloping ground as she travelled deeper before making a slow rise back up. Soon an opening appeared in the distance. The glow of light became brighter and brighter as the tunnel sloped downward once more. At the end of it, she squinted. Her eyes adjusted, and she stood stunned. She was at the mouth of a cave. Before her was a lush green valley and running further along was a stream. She stepped out and stared around her, shifting her attention high atop the meadow that rose to her east. Glenhaven stood tall and proud before her in the distance, and the valley she had spied yesterday stood just beyond her below. Animals roamed and grazed the hillside in the distance, and small cottages dotted the landscape. It was breathtaking.

'I see you made it.'

Ewan.

Catriona whipped around and saw Laird Stewart standing behind her. 'Where did you come from?' she asked, scanning the area.

He pointed to an outcropping. 'Just beyond the rocks. Since I missed giving you a tour yesterday, I thought we'd go for a ride today, so I can show you the lands under my care. I thought it might help you to see what a laird does and therefore what his wife might also be responsible for.'

Ack.

She hesitated and pulled at her fingertips. While she expected it would come up at some point, she did not know it would be today. 'I do not ride, my laird.'

He balked, his eyes widening. 'You do not like to ride?' he asked, disbelief in his tone.

'Nay. Well, I do not know if I like to ride or not. I never learned.' Heat warmed her cheeks and neck. She smoothed her skirts to attempt to soften her embarrassment. Not knowing how to ride was akin to poverty.

'Oh,' he answered.

'There was no need for me to learn. I have never had a horse or known anyone who could afford their own. Well, except for the Chisholms, and they never allowed staff to ride their horses.'

'Do you wish to learn?'

She shrugged. 'Perhaps,' she said, trying to shake off the uncertainty filling her from her toes to her hair. 'Where did you wish to ride to?'

He pointed above and behind her. 'Up through the valley and along the borders. As much as I can show you of our lands in the time we have today.'

Her stomach lurched. *Blast.* How would she manage a horse on her own throughout these sections of rock and inclines? And what of the descents? She balked.

She wouldn't.

'Or I can have the stable hand return your mount to the barn, and we can ride together?' Ewan offered.

''Tis your choice, but is too far to walk, and I do wish you to see the land.'

She hesitated and then gave in. 'I will ride with you, then.'

He smiled. 'I will let the lad know and return with our mount. Wait here.'

As if there was anywhere else she would go.

This is a new adventure. Take a deep breath. You can do this. He will be just like a carriage horse.

Ewan returned, leading the largest horse she had ever seen in all her days. *Curses.* This dark, looming stallion was no carriage horse. It was an impressive creature that could toss her from its back at its whim or crush her beneath its sizable hooves in a heartbeat. Catriona took a step back as Ewan brought the horse to where she was standing.

'This is Wee Bit,' he stated, rubbing the horse's nose, which was as dark as black tar.

She scoffed. 'You named him *Wee Bit*?'

He smiled. 'Nay. I didn't, but the stableman's son did. The lad has a keen sense of humour.'

'I can see that,' she murmured, not that she found any humour in it now.

'Come. Don't be afraid. Give him a pat so he can smell you. It will put you both at ease.'

'And if he doesn't take to me?'

'We'll find that out rather quickly,' he said with a wink, brushing his hair off his forehead.

She rolled her eyes at him. 'Just the words to give me courage.' She stepped forward and approached the large beast, focusing on slow and steady movements that wouldn't scare the horse or her. Then she put her splayed palm out to the horse's snout. Ewan reached out and quickly squeezed her fingers together. 'You want to cup your palm with your fingers close together, so he won't accidentally bite one off.'

'Blazes,' she murmured, her heart hammering in her chest.

He chuckled at her curse. 'Just trust him…and me.' He met her gaze and held it. She nodded and released a breath. Then Wee Bit nuzzled her hand.

Ewan pulled a piece of apple from his coat pocket and placed it in her palm, the faint skim of the coarse pads of his fingertips against her skin igniting a trail of awareness. The horse gobbled up the apple slice from her hand a second later. The tickle of hair from its whiskers and sweep of its tongue on her palm made her laugh. Ewan smiled. 'See?'

She reached up and dared pet its snout. The stallion leaned into her hand, and she savoured his sweet acceptance, as it was a mirror of Ewan's own. 'He's gentle,' she whispered.

'Aye. He may look like a beast, but he is a gentle giant.'

'Like you?'

'I suppose,' he answered, looking away.

'It isn't a flaw to be kind, my laird.'

'In these parts, it might as well be. The people are used to my father.' He ran a hand absent-mindedly down the neck of Wee Bit. 'Bran Stewart was a hard, demanding, and unyielding laird, and they respected him for it. But I cannot be that man, for I am not him. And when

I attempt to be, well, I just look like an arse *trying* to be a laird, not actually a laird at all.'

'Then don't be your father. Be yourself.'

He stilled and met her gaze. His Adam's apple bobbed in his throat as he swallowed. 'You believe the people would accept me if I were myself and not like my father?' The urgency of his question revealed his desperation to her, and her heart squeezed at the realisation of it. Even a laird such as Ewan struggled to find his way in the world. It wasn't just her, and that knowing brought her a sense of peace. Maybe she didn't have to know everything right now. She didn't have to be keen on an escape from this place and from him just yet. She could stay her two weeks and try to figure out what she wanted. For once, she could embrace the time she was given and enjoy it without fear.

She risked the truth. 'Aye. I think it's possible. I can't predict how they would react, but from what I know about men, you seem a good one, and that should count for something. Should it not?'

Bollocks.

Ewan squeezed the reins in his hands, feeling the leather tattoo his skin, but he held fast. It was the only thing keeping him from kissing the life out of her. If the woman didn't stop saying things like that, things that made him feel seen, things that made him want to be a better man, to be the man she believed he was, he wouldn't be able to walk away from her. Worse yet, he wouldn't be able to stop himself from loving her. The longer she set her beautiful amber eyes upon him, so full of expectation and belief, the more alive he felt, and the more drawn to her he was. But part of him knew that he was the moth to her flame, and that opening himself up to her would be allowing himself to be consumed entire. He'd scarce survived losing Emogene. He wouldn't survive a loss as heavy as that a second time.

'I wish goodness mattered here in the Highlands,' he replied, cutting his eyes away from her, 'but I don't think kindness will keep you alive. Only exerting power and control will.'

Hurt flashed in her eyes before she glanced away, and he knew he'd done what he'd needed to: kept his distance. If they married, they would be happier without the vice of love to squeeze the very life out of them. The sooner she knew that, the better off they could be. He pulled up on his mount and settled back in the saddle.

'Care to join me?' he asked, reaching out an open hand to her, attempting to lighten the mood he had just squashed to bits.

She lifted her gaze and bit her lip, a tell of her nerves he was beginning to recognise. 'How do I?' She gestured to him and the saddle.

'Put your shoe in the stirrup, grab my hand, and I'll hoist you up in front of me.'

Her gaze went from the stirrup to his hand to the horse, and she stepped back, shaking her head. 'I don't think...'

'Is it that you do not trust me, or the horse?'

When she didn't answer, he knew what she was thinking: both.

'I promise I won't let you fall.'

She closed her eyes and let out a deep breath. Then she shoved her boot in the stirrup and grabbed his extended hand, and he pulled her up. She was so light that she almost flew right back off the saddle after she landed in front of him, but he gripped her waist in time to bring her back to centre.

She clutched his thigh to steady herself, and he stifled a groan. Perhaps this wasn't the best of ideas. She smelled of something light and floral that he couldn't name, and the wisps of hair escaping her plait ran like silk threads against his cheek. This ride would drive him mad, and yet he craved the madness it would stir within him, just like that moth and its flame. The warmer she felt against him, the closer he wanted her, even though he knew in some deeper, faraway place that it would never be close enough.

'Ready?' he asked, his voice far huskier than he intended.

She released his thigh and clutched the horn of the saddle so tightly he feared it might be crushed to dust. 'Aye,' she said, even though it sounded more like a question than an answer.

With a click of his tongue and his heel, they were off at a slow trot along the valley. After travelling several minutes in silence, she finally relaxed against him.

'This is the valley where we used to play as children.' He couldn't keep the mirth from his voice. 'Even though it would start as a game of hide and find, Moira always allowed herself to be found first so she could sit among the flowers. She always loved botany and would bore me to tears with her explanations of what plants could be used for and where they grew best. Strange how I miss such talks now.'

The sun was climbing high in the sky, its rays chasing away the chill of the morn as they continued. He paused at the crest of the hill and pointed out to the horizon. 'Do you see our men far off in the distance working along the stone wall?'

She leaned forward. 'Aye.'

'Our lands run up until the wall we share with the MacGregors. If you follow that wall, it wraps along the edges of the borders we share with the Camerons as well.'

'It is impressive.'

'And thousands of men, women, and children depend on us keeping it that way.'

'Surely you don't place that burden solely on your own shoulders? One man cannot keep a clan thriving and in order. It is the responsibility of all to maintain such things.' She spoke with a certainty that made him smile.

'If only all had such a belief.' He clicked his tongue, and Wee Bit carried on to the south end, slowing as they descended a section of rocks and small boulders. Catriona slid forward in the saddle and gasped in alarm.

'Steady,' he murmured. He wrapped one arm around her waist as he gripped the reins with the other. He was startled by the slightness of her form. To know she was so fearful of riding was an odd contrast to all that she had endured and the strength he knew she possessed. The land levelled out, and she relaxed in his hold. He loosened his arm around her all too soon.

As they roamed, he pointed out the cottages clustered about the various farming, mining, sheering, livestock, and herbal centres of the clan. Many of the men and women stopped their work to greet them, while others watched with suspicion, wondering no doubt about why he travelled with a woman who was a stranger to them.

Little did they know the importance of it. Mrs Catriona Gordon might very well become his wife.

Chapter Fourteen

"'Tis a glorious thing to have my feet settled back on the ground,' Catriona stated. Her sides tingled from where Ewan had just released his hold about her waist after helping her dismount from Wee Bit. She stroked the large horse's nose. 'And *you* were quite gentle, kind sir, as your master promised.'

'You see, you did not perish during your ride.' Ewan smiled as he passed the reins off to the stable boy. 'Take good care of him, Reed,' he told the young lad. 'Extra oats for him this eve,' he added with a wink.

'Aye, me laird,' the boy answered with a smile and nod. 'My lady,' he offered with a small bow before he led the horse off to be brushed down.

'You are right,' Catriona answered. 'I indeed did not perish, although I did imagine myself toppling off the horse and careening down a few of the hillsides as we travelled.'

'I would never let any harm come to you,' he said. And the way he spoke the words made her heart twist and turn, as if it too wished to believe his words but didn't quite trust them.

She pressed her lips together.

He nodded. 'Slow to trust?'

'Perhaps.'

'Then, we are a well-matched pair,' he jested as he brushed dirt from his trews.

It was now or never.

She squared her shoulders. 'I gathered that from last night. I am sorry I pushed you. It was not my place to enquire about something so personal, especially when we really do not know one another.' The apology fell stiffly from her lips, but she meant it.

He stilled and met her gaze. 'And I am sorry as well. I should not have acted like an arse with my answer.' He shrugged and sighed. 'I have not spoken about her to anyone in a long time.'

'I understand. There is much pain from my past that I choose to keep close to me rather than share, which makes me an arse for expecting you to share your own so freely.'

He chuckled. 'I was angry, but only due to the feeling it brought up for me. Shame more than anything. I went against my clan, my father, and an alliance, all for her, because I believed she loved me.'

She waited for him to continue.

'We were to marry, but in the end, she married a Sutherland. All because he had more power, more coin. It was a hard lesson for me to learn.'

'What lesson was that?'

'That love is not always enough.'

'Ah. So that was the reason for your no-love clause in your proposal to me? To prevent such misfortune again?'

'Aye. It is to protect us both.'

'Thank you for telling me, so that I could understand.'

He shrugged. 'If we are to wed, then you should know what you're getting into,' he said with a smirk.

'I suppose you are right.'

'I thought you might like to walk down to the loch. Are you up to it?' he asked.

'Aye. It sounds glorious. I'll have a chance to stretch my legs after the ride and remind myself of what it feels like to have my feet fully anchored to the ground.'

He laughed. 'The riding will become easier. And the first time you let your horse free across an open field, you will love it. I know you will.'

'You do?' Did he claim to know her already? Her pulse increased.

He nodded. 'Aye. I do. You have spirit, Mrs Gordon, and didn't you say you crave freedom?'

'Aye.'

'Well, there is not much that compares to the freedom you feel riding full out on your own mount across an open field with the sun beaming on your face and the wind whipping through your hair. I hope I get to see that moment. That will be a sight to behold.'

She sucked in an unsteady breath. The way he looked at her, as if he knew things about her that she did not even know about herself, sent every fibre of her being aflame. It also made her long to know what would set him free as well.

'And you, my laird, what is it that would set your spirit free?' She walked alongside him, her fingertips accidentally skimming the back of his hand for the briefest of touches.

He paused.

'Honestly?' he asked, stepping closer.

'Aye,' she whispered.

'Kissing you.'

Her breath hitched in her throat, and she swallowed hard. 'Then why don't you?'

He stared devilishly at her lips as if they were water itself before meeting her gaze. 'Well, we do not know if you are still married to Mr Gordon or not. And you have already told me that you do not trust yourself around me, so if *I* do not hold the line on our attraction to one another, we will be in dire shape, will we not? And I know I couldn't stop myself at one kiss.'

His gaze held images of such abandon, and she released a breath. 'Then I am grateful for your restraint,' she answered, leaning forward until her breath blew across his cheek. 'Let us see how long it holds for both of us.'

She stepped back and began to walk down the hillside towards the loch below, its waters dark and rippling. This playful banter between them was something she'd never had before, and she found she liked it far more than she wished to admit. She also knew she was playing with fire. One false move and they might both be consumed.

Deuces.

Ewan rubbed the back of his neck and ruffled his hair. If anyone had told him a week ago that he would find a woman to become his wife and burn with attraction for her as well, Ewan would have laughed aloud at them and sent for the doctor to have them checked for fever. But it was true. He'd felt more alive with Mrs Gordon in these last few days than he had felt in years. His steps faltered.

More alive than he had felt since losing Emogene.

While he knew he should be tending to his duties as laird this afternoon, all he wanted was to spend more time with Mrs Gordon. To learn what made her laugh, to know the secrets of her heart, the pain that had shaped her into who she was today. All in all, he was acting like a lovesick fool, and despite the terror that elicited in him, there was a small seed of wonder growing in his gut.

Could he have love like Moira and Brenna had and not be consumed by it? Was he doomed to a life of plodding along one foot in front of the other as laird, or could he also have happiness? Hell, could Catriona help him become a better man, be the laird he wished to be? She had a way of pushing him and challenging him that he admired, and yet she also possessed a directness that relaxed him.

He followed her down the hillside, watching her take those first steps onto the craggy shore. A smile played on her lips as she turned to him, her hair whipping in the breeze, the sun setting her face aglow. And wasn't she turning into some other woman each day she stayed here? She was far from the tattered lass who didn't dare make eye contact with him at the start of their journey in the carriage from Edinburgh to Glasgow. Each day, more light came into her eyes and her spirit, as if she too had been hidden from the world and perhaps from herself.

Together, they seemed to be finding one another. And it was equally compelling and terrifying.

He reached the shore and stood alongside her on the grey rocks that filled the coastline. For minutes they just looked out at the loch in silence, water rolling in along the shoals, the rhythmic ebb and flow of the small tide and smell of the water filling his senses.

'It is incredibly peaceful here,' she said.

'Aye.'

'I have few memories of my childhood,' she offered, staring out into the dark waters. 'But the strongest one is of being on a beach. I can smell the sea, feel the warm sand between my toes and the sun heating my arms and face. I remember laughing with my siblings, being teased by one of my brothers, and then chasing him and the waves along the shore.'

'That is all you remember?'

'And being swallowed by the waves, desperately trying to reach the surface for air, and failing.' She shivered. 'I also remember snippets of things.' She bent to pick up a small pebble, freckled with minerals but smoothed by the sea. 'I remember finding a piece of sea glass that day, a vibrant blue-green. Your eyes reminded me of it when we first met.'

He tucked his hands in his pockets to keep from touching her. 'What happened to it?'

'I don't have any idea. I remember finding it and showing it to my brother.'

'Do you ever wonder what happened to them? Your siblings. Your parents. Why they did not come to find you, claim you?' His questions tumbled out before he could think better of it. After all, it wasn't his business, was it?

'Every day,' she answered without pause as she threw the pebble far out into the loch.

He understood the anguish in her voice and the pull of insanity such a daily thought was. It was how he thought upon the death of his mother and the betrayal of Emogene, even though the losses were dissimilar. They still caused pain as open wounds that couldn't be healed, much like her own.

'Now, who is poking their finger into an open wound and expecting a bloody answer?' Her words hit him like tiny barbs lancing his skin. She faced him. Her features were pinched, pained even, and he wished he hadn't asked, that he could gather his words back and hide them away, but he couldn't.

'I did not mean…' he murmured, uncertain how to continue.

'You did not mean to ask me the truth? No doubt, you did.'

He nodded. 'You are right. I am sorry.'

'I believe I've had my fill of fresh air,' she replied.

'I'll escort you back,' he offered.

'I can find my own way, my laird,' she answered, lifting her skirts and starting up the incline. He watched her go, knowing that he had placed a wedge between them after all the connection they had just built, and he couldn't help but wonder if he'd done it intentionally to keep her at bay.

For the prospect of loving anyone was a scary venture, especially the thought of daring to care for a woman as enchanting and mesmerising as Mrs Catriona Gordon.

Chapter Fifteen

The man was working her temper into a fine boil. Catriona climbed the hillside and drew in long breaths to calm the anger brewing. His simple questions shouldn't create so much ire in her, but they did. Most likely because she also wanted answers to them, and she had for years. Why hadn't her parents come for her? Did they not love her enough to search for her? Had they given up so easily? Why?

Perhaps she wasn't good enough.

Mr Arran's cruel words echoed in her head. *'Ye be nothin', lass. That's why yer parents never claimed ye.'*

The familiar shame at the thought of it being true emerged, and her chest constricted. She could not hold the feeling for long before she wished to simply scream.

Blast.

The man could drive a sane woman to the asylum.

She huffed out a breath, picking up speed as she climbed. The burn of exertion to her legs and body felt delicious because she hadn't been working as hard as her body was used to doing for days now. She'd have to discover some outlet for all her excess energy, or she might just murder the man over the coming weeks until her departure.

Departure?

She faltered. Did she truly want to leave?

At this moment she did, but what of later when her anger cooled? In the last few days, she had been cared for, laughed, met kind people, and explored more new facets of herself and the world than she had in the last decade.

But she could also be free. The wind whipped up around her, and she snuggled deeper in her shawl. A storm was blowing in, and soon there would be a downpour. She hustled up the remaining distance to the castle and entered through the side door. Soon Betsy intercepted her.

'Did ye enjoy yer time with the laird?' she asked, falling into step with Catriona.

She paused. 'Aye. I enjoyed the tour of the lands. I could have done without the enquiry that came along with it,' she huffed. There was no use in keeping her anger hidden. Betsy was no fool.

To Catriona's surprise, Betsy smirked. 'Is that so?' she asked.

'Aye. 'Tis so.' She dropped her voice. 'The man could drive a nun to murder, I tell you.'

Betsy smothered a laugh. 'Let us get ye changed. The elders will be joining ye for dinner.'

'They are?'

Betsy shifted on her feet. 'The laird said he would

mention it to ye, but perhaps with all that has happened…' her words trailed off.

Catriona frowned.

'Best ye work through that temper before they arrive. Perhaps a hot bath would do the trick?' Betsy offered with a smile.

Catriona sighed aloud. 'Aye. That sounds heavenly.'

'Say no more. I will let the other servants know, so they can begin heating the water, and then I'll return shortly to help ye out of yer gown.'

She gave Betsy's arm a quick squeeze. 'Thank you.'

With her spirit lifted at the thought of yet another hot bath, Catriona hurried along the corridor to her chambers. As she reached her door and set her hand on the knob to open it, she stopped cold at the sound of a footman speaking with Mrs Stevens down the hallway.

'Correspondence from the solicitor has arrived,' he said. 'Instructions were that I was to hand it directly to the laird and only the laird.'

'Hmm. Ye may be in for a long wait, lad. He's not returned yet from his travels along the borders with Mrs Gordon.'

'Should I leave it in his study then? I've many a chore to do before dinner with the elders this eve.'

'Aye. Head on. I'll leave it on his desk in the study. No one should bother it. I'll send him in to look upon it as soon as he arrives.'

'Aye, ma'am.'

Following the sound of footfalls and a door opening and closing, Catriona stood still, deciding on what to do. She *could* sneak in and peek at that letter, or she could leave it be. He would tell her the contents one way or the other, wouldn't he? But if she opened it, he might know what she'd done.

Or she could reseal it and he would never know. Well, he might not know.

Or she might break his trust entirely.

Would it matter?

Ack.

The thoughts in her mind were akin to a game of keep away. Why could she not decide whether she wished to stay or go, or care for the man or despise him? And why could he also not decide whether he cared for or despised her?

Before she could think longer upon any of those things, she needed to decide if she would sneak into his study and look upon the letter or not. Betsy would return soon, and then her option would evaporate. She gave in to the devil upon her shoulder and snuck down the hallway, careful to see if anyone was coming her way. Even though she was the laird's guest, her snooping about in the study alone would not be well received. So far, the corridor was empty. No doubt many of the servants were busy preparing the meal and dining room for the arrival of the elders which the laird had failed to mention to her.

She grumbled under her breath and set her handle upon the study door. She turned the knob, and it easily gave way. The door hadn't even been locked. *Blazes.* What had she even been worried about?

'Mrs Gordon,' the laird said behind her, his tone

smooth and curious. 'Were you looking for me so soon after our outing? I must say I am surprised.'

Catriona stilled, clenched her jaw, and cursed under her breath. What was he doing back already, and how on earth had she not heard his approach? She let go of the handle, set a tight smile to her face, and turned to him. When she saw his feet were clad only in his stockings, she knew exactly how she hadn't heard him. The man had no shoes on.

She lifted her brow as she looked upon his soiled stockings.

He shrugged. 'Stepped in a large mud hole near the barn when I went to see Wee Bit. Mrs Stevens kindly asked me to leave them on the steps out of doors.'

'Aye,' she answered. 'I thought you would be some time still.'

'Oh? Did you have need of me already? Here I was thinking you were angry at me.' He flashed a rogue smile at her as if he were all too pleased with himself and her visit.

She wanted to crown the man, but she decided to seize her advantage instead. The best defence was to have a strong attack, so she pulled from what little she had in her arsenal. She crossed her arms against her chest. 'Aye. Betsy informed me that we were dining with the elders tonight. Was there a point in time that you were going to let me know that, so I could prepare? How are you even going to introduce me?'

His smile faltered, and he cringed. 'Aye. I did forget to tell you. I did not think upon it as we were out this morn.' He ran a hand through his hair. 'Come in. Let us speak of it now.' He pushed the door open for her and followed her inside.

'Betsy will be bringing along water for a hot bath for me shortly, so…' She lingered near the door.

He studied her. 'Are you still angry?' he asked.

'Aye, my laird. I am.'

He sighed and sank down in the chair before his desk. 'I did not intend harm in my question. I wanted to know so that I could understand, not shame you.' He lifted the letter on his desk and scanned the writing, momentarily distracted by it before he set it aside. No doubt it was *the* letter she was desperate to know the contents of, yet he seemed to have little interest in it. *Odd.*

'Understand what?' she countered. 'There is no mystery in how you found me. Isn't that all you need to know of my past?' A flush heated her cheeks. Now that she had set some of her anger and frustration free, it was quite hard to wrestle it down. Her pulse increased, and she couldn't slow her breathing.

'I asked so I could be better at…' He paused searching for the right word before he gave up. 'Better at being your husband if it comes to that, and understanding what might be hard for you to adjust to here as my wife. There was no malice in my enquiry, despite what you may believe.' He met her gaze.

'Even though I may decide to leave you?'

He frowned. 'Aye. Even then.' He interlocked his fingers and sat back in his chair. 'As you may have guessed, I am not used to opening up to people. My attempts have been clumsy, but there is no ill intent.'

She wiggled her toes in her slippers. What did one say to that?

'Oh,' she replied and pressed her lips together in a fine line of regret.

'As for our dinner this eve,' he began, ploughing on to a new topic before this one had been anywhere near resolved, 'you will meet the elders. What do you wish to know about them before they arrive, so you can be ready?'

'Now that I think on it, it may be best that you tell me nothing, so I can have a clear and untainted view of them and their intentions. However, I do need to know what story you shall give them about me.'

'As we discussed as a possibility before, I will tell them you are Garrick's long-lost cousin who is staying with us while his own castle is under repairs, which is true, so that you can be comfortable, but also have time to get to know his new wife-to-be, my sister, of course.'

'And Laird MacLean and Brenna have agreed to this?'

'Aye. They have.'

'Then, I look forward to our dinner and observing what exactly these men are up to.'

'I will see you at eight then,' he said.

She walked towards the door, and as her foot hit the threshold, he called to her.

'And Mrs Gordon, if you ever want to know what is in my library, you can always just ask.' He winked at her and then turned away before she could answer.

Blast. The man had known what she was up to from the start. If only she knew exactly what *he* was up to.

* * *

'You made quite the impression this eve, Mrs Gordon,' said Ewan as he returned to the dining room, having escorted the elders out for the evening. She had quite affected him as well. The woman surprised him every moment she spent with him, and those surprises spoke to his soul in a way he didn't wish to acknowledge as he became more and more attracted to her.

Even in profile, she was astounding, and he shored himself up against it as best he could, which wasn't very well at all. 'Were you as interested as you seemed in our discussions?' he asked, attempting to keep their conversation on neutral ground.

Catriona turned away from the windows and faced him, the candlelight catching the shadows and light across her face. 'Almost,' she replied.

'As I suspected.' He scanned the room. 'Where did Brenna go?'

'She retired. Something about being bored for so long that she might as well go to bed.' She chuckled, and the small locket at her throat winked at him in the glow of the wall sconces.

'I cannot say I blame her,' he added. 'Once Niven begins, it is quite hard for him to end.'

'However, he could be your greatest asset,' she stated, lifting her brow at him. Her words stopped him in his tracks.

'Are we speaking of the same man?'

'Aye. The eldest of them. The one who appears to be the hardest on you wants you dearly to succeed. I can see it in the way he looks at you. But Broden...he is quite a different story. Envy shines in his eyes when you speak. He wishes to have everything you possess. *He* is the one I would watch out for. He is an opportunist, and he is waiting for a chance to unseat you to arise.'

'That does not surprise me. He was angry when I did not give him rein over the soldiers for I did not believe him skilled enough to train them. And Harris?' Ewan asked, unable to wait a moment longer for her thoughts on him.

She shrugged. 'Perhaps a nuisance, but he is no threat. I believe he will take the path of least resistance, whatever that may be. He seemed to shift allegiances as the conversation went on. No doubt that is his plan moving forward. He may be an ally or a foe.'

'You decided all of this from one eve with them over one meal?' Ewan frowned at her. 'How can you be certain?'

Her fingertips trailed over the rim of her wine glass until it sang under her touch. A sweet high-pitched tone that filled the room. Once she ceased and it faded away, she met his gaze and held it. 'Because in my experience, making a mistake in the judgement of a man can cost you your life. So, aye, I am sure. And in exchange for this help I have provided you, I would like to know what was in the letter today that you went to great pains to make me believe held little or no significance despite its importance to me…and to you.'

He smirked. 'Interesting. You mean from my solicitor?'

She nodded.

He tilted his head. 'And you would know that he sent

me a letter, how? You do not know his script. Even that is beyond your skill set, I believe.'

'Aye, it is. I do not know his penmanship, but I over-heard your footman bring it in, and upon being unable to find you, Mrs Stevens bid him leave it on your desk. He was quite reluctant to do so as that went against the messenger's orders, but he did it anyway. Mrs Stevens can be quite persuasive.'

'Ahh. So now I know why you were attempting to enter my study.'

She did not confirm or deny his assertion, which was an affirmation of her intentions if there ever was one, the little minx. He should have been angry but found himself intrigued by her boldness and ingenuity instead.

'I have not opened it,' he offered. He sipped from his wine glass and set it aside on the mantel.

She approached him, narrowing her eyes. 'I do not know if I believe you.'

'You cannot read me after all our time together? That I find interesting, especially after your speech about the importance of being able to read people to protect oneself.' He walked closer to her. 'Do you not see the answer in my eyes?'

She stood in silent assessment of him, her gaze slowly scanning his face, the light catching those gold and moss specks in her amber irises and her shoulders rising and falling delicately with each breath. The lavender gown she wore this eve was quite devastating against her pale skin, and her hair was swept artfully into a low knot at the nape of her neck. How he would kiss that neck if he could.

She smirked just then as if she could read his thoughts, and heat flushed along his neck. *Deuces*. He hoped she wasn't *that* good at reading people.

'I believe you. Let us open it now, then, so I can know my fate. It is important to know which husband you are married to, is it not?' She laughed and set her glass down before boldly clasping his hand in hers and tugging him along to follow.

The feel of her hand in his sent a bolt of fire through his body, and he held on fiercely. He caught up and then challenged her to match his pace as they jogged down the corridor to his study. Her laughter filled his ears as he let go of her hand at the doorway and went in. As he strode to the desk, he realised how desperately he wanted to be her husband. How much he craved to claim her as his own.

And how much he feared all he felt for her, as she could leave him even now. The realisation soured his throat. She had power over him. He hesitated, but then took the letter in hand.

'Well, go on then. Do not leave me wondering. Am I still Mrs Gordon, or am I now Lady Stewart?'

He set his mask in place as he popped open the heavy wax seal of the letter from his solicitor. He scanned its contents and then set it on the desk before slumping down in the chair and releasing a curse.

'You are disappointed I am your bride?' she teased.

'I do not know anything for certain, nor do you. See for yourself.' He tossed the letter across the table and set his boots up on the corner of the desk, crossing them at the ankles.

Why could nothing be easy?

She picked it up and read it before setting it back down and sitting in the seat across from him. 'What exactly does *more time* mean, do you think? A day, a week, a month?'

'A good question. It seems he will let us know the moment he hears something more official, but until then, he is unsure whether what happened in the Grassmarket was a legal contract or not and whether you are my wife or not. He cannot be certain until he completes more enquiries of his own.'

'That's rather grey, isn't it?'

'Aye,' he said, resting his head against the back of the chair, 'it is.'

'So now what do we do, merely wait?'

'Do you have other ideas?' he asked.

'Nay, my laird. But what if the answer takes longer than our two-week trial? What will we do then?'

'Perhaps we should just take it a day at a time. Then, once we reach the end of our two weeks, we can decide.'

She shrugged. 'I suppose that is as good of an idea as any…as is going to bed.' She stood and stretched her arms over her head, looking every bit like a cat stretching her sleek limbs high in the air. He swallowed hard. Too bad her latest statement had not been an invitation. He would have accepted it in an instant.

'Thank you for your help with the elders this eve. I would never have deduced their intentions in such a way. I hope you will teach me your methods.'

'Much of it cannot be taught, my laird. You must

learn to trust your instincts, your gut, that small voice in the back of your head that tells you the truth.'

He sat up, settling his feet back on the floor. 'I am not sure I know what you mean.'

'Then perhaps that shall be my lesson for you tomorrow. After you finish your meetings in the morn, meet me at the stables.'

'The stables?'

She nodded.

'I will see you there.'

'I bid you a good eve and good sleep, my laird.'

'And to you, Mrs Gordon.'

'And be sure to wear something you don't mind getting a bit dirty tomorrow morn for our lessons,' she said. She smiled, and the twinkle of playful mischief was back in her eyes. He found he could scarce wait to see what plans she had in store for him. Each day with this lass was an adventure. He felt more alive than he had in ages, and it scared the blazes out of him.

Chapter Sixteen

'I am here as requested,' Ewan stated.

Catriona turned to face the barn door and smiled. 'I am pleased to see you eager for your lesson today, my laird.' She glanced at his worn tunic and trews. 'And that you came prepared to get a bit dirty.'

Anticipation raced through him. While he found he wasn't always one to enjoy surprises, he did enjoy hers. He lifted his brows. 'Eager may be an overstatement. I am more curious as to how you will teach me the ways of men in the stables, of all places.' And how he would manage to focus on her lessons. She wore a plain brown dress rather than one of Brenna's frocks and found the simplicity of the cut quite flattering. Her hair was also pulled back in a long singular plait, which showcased the beauty of her face.

'You look quite lovely this morn,' he said.

She paused her work and blushed. 'Thank you. Betsy was kind enough to loan me a day dress so I would not soil another one of Brenna's gowns.' She lifted a bale of hay and plopped it near the barn door. 'Have a seat,' she said, patting the bale with her hand.

He came over to the bale and sat as requested. 'Now, close your eyes,' she said.

He frowned. 'Why?'

'Because it is the first part of my lesson for you this morn. Eyes. Closed.'

'Hopefully it will not be my last,' he muttered and then closed his eyes.

'I am blindfolding you for this first part.'

'Isn't the whole point for me to learn how to read cues from people based on what I see? How can I do that if I am blindfolded?'

'Seeing is only one part of understanding someone and their intentions.' She cinched the scrap of cloth around his eyes tightly. 'Shush.'

He captured one of her hands in his own and kissed the tips of her fingers. 'In case this is my last chance to kiss you,' he chuckled.

She wriggled her fingertips away. 'You will not perish unless you continue to complain.'

He smothered a smile.

'Now, I want you to sit quietly and tell me everything you hear.'

'What?'

'Please just try it.'

He took a deep breath and released it. Then, he listened. 'I hear some rustling in the barn, most likely from the animals, mixed with some of your impatience with me.'

'I am quite sure you can do better than that,' she called, some distance from him now.

'Aye.' He listened again, taking pains to truly try. 'I hear the leaves in the breeze. Also, an animal drinking water, perhaps a goat or dog. And now I hear footsteps approaching me, most likely you.'

'That is better. Now tell me what you smell.'

He wrinkled his nose. 'Definitely hay, manure, dirt, and perhaps a tinge of a sweet-smelling soap from you.'

'Now extend your hands, and tell me what you feel.'

He smiled at the feel of fur beneath his touch. 'A goat, but I could have deduced that by its scent.'

He heard her walk away and then back to him.

'Good. And what about now?'

A slobbering kiss lathered his hand and he laughed. 'Rufus.'

'Aye. Perhaps too easy. Now, imagine what you already know about the layout of the barn and walk to my voice. Careful though. I may have placed some obstacles in your path.'

He stood and frowned. 'How on earth is any of this helping me to read people?'

'Tsk tsk, my laird. Just try.'

'How shall I ever reach you if you are moving?'

'Ah! Very good. You see, you are improving already. You can tell I am moving from you and not in a fixed spot. Keep walking to me. But take care to mind your steps.'

'Why do I feel this is a trial of humiliation rather than a lesson in deciphering behaviour?' He reached out his arms and felt around him but didn't touch anything. Then he stumbled over an object beneath his feet. Though he saved himself from falling, it was not without a curse.

'Keep going, my laird.'

After an additional stagger over what may or may not have been a broom handle, he slowed his steps, walking carefully. He listened for hints of where he was, imagined the interior of the barn he had been in thousands of times, and sniffed occasionally to see if he was moving further away from her or closer to her. That sweet floral scent of hers was intoxicating. He kicked over a bucket with a thud and paused. Finally, he took another step, reached out his hand, and touched Catriona's arm.

'Well done. You may remove your blindfold,' she said.

Ewan released his hold on her forearm and tugged off the blindfold. He glanced back to see he had travelled across a large section of the barn floor that had been scattered with objects. He counted himself lucky not to have stepped on the trio of eggs on the ground. He frowned. 'So, what was the point of such an exercise?'

'To be in the moment, use your senses, and to trust yourself and your instincts more. For example, you began to stop, listen, and gauge your steps more carefully. You were present to your surroundings, assessing where you were, where I was, and how to reach me safely.'

'I was?'

'Aye. My hope is this will serve as a reminder for you to trust your instincts. Everyone has them. You seem to always doubt yours, except for that day in the market. You set aside your doubts and acted on pure instinct.

You rescued me and trusted me enough to ride for two days in a carriage with me.'

'I believe that was more madness.'

'Was it? Or were you allowing your heart, your gut, your instincts to drive you into action to save me? And if you had not done that, I might very well be dead.'

He swallowed hard. Imagining her dead, not here with him, made his heart thunder in his chest and the blood in his body constrict.

She took both of his hands in hers. 'Let yourself feel. Listening to the part of you that gives you instinct will also give you insight, but you have to allow it to come to the surface. Your emotion, your kindness, your care, your love…that is what you must harness to be able to read the motivations of others better. You cannot know those things about others if you do not know them of yourself. I believe you are best when you listen to yourself, follow that heart of yours you seem so keen to set aside, and trust your instincts about people. What you believe to be a special skill I possess is merely self-reliance. Everyone has it, even you. But you must allow yourself to feel it, even when it is uncomfortable.'

He held her gaze, and something shifted deep inside him, as if her words played a song in his heart that he had waited his whole life to hear. This woman felt he was enough as he was. He was not lacking. He did not need extra skill, but more self-belief.

He needed to believe in himself like she did.

He swallowed hard, emotion and confusion clouding his mind. He narrowed his gaze at her. 'Are you telling me you believe I could have deciphered what you did about the elders at our dinner by paying more attention and trusting my instincts?'

'Aye. I believe you could decipher more about everyone if you did those things.'

He shook his head. 'I don't think so.'

'Why not? You have such skills with animals. I have seen you ride Wee Bit. You two communicate with each other and trust each other. That is based on you using your senses to know what you can and cannot do together as horse and rider. If you applied that same confidence and belief in yourself when you met with the clan leaders and elders, you would know who you could count on and trust as part of your inner circle and who you couldn't.'

A knock sounded on the frame of the barn door. 'Are you ready for your ride today, Mrs Gordon?' Hewe asked. The clan's most skilled horse trainer and rider glanced around at the random items all over the barn floor.

Catriona let go of Ewan's hands, and a sweet flush rose into her neck. 'I did not realise the time. I am sure the laird is ready to be done with my mischief.' She smiled. 'I will clean up and join you shortly.'

'Aye, Mrs Gordon. I'll ready yer mount.' Hewe headed out.

Catriona picked up a few of the scattered items and returned them to their shelves and racks. Ewan silently assisted her until they were done. Although he desperately wished to talk, he couldn't. He didn't know what exactly to say. He had so many questions, and so many uncertainties.

'Can it be so simple?' he asked, placing the trio of eggs in the small bowl she held.

'Aye, my laird. It can.' Her eyes were steady and clear.

'Your certainty is something I wish dearly I possessed.'

She shrugged. 'Then choose it, Ewan. There is no secret in it. Trust yourself. I do.'

And with that, she handed him the bowl of eggs, pressed a kiss to his cheek, and left the barn humming the clarsach melody.

Ewan stood frozen, wondering what had just happened and why everything that seemed so impossible without Catriona seemed so bloody possible with her.

Chapter Seventeen

'A letter from the solicitor has arrived.'

Catriona glanced up from the settee to see Ewan leaning on the door frame of her chamber. She smiled at the sight of him. He looked devilishly handsome with his mussed black hair, rolled shirt sleeves, and loosened cravat, all signs that he had been hard at work poring over maps or the account books for the clan when the letter arrived.

She put the pressed flower he'd given her from one of her first nights here on the page of the book she was reading to keep her place and closed it gently. The adventures of Cecilia and William would have to wait for another day, it seemed. She sat up, tucked her stocking feet under herself, and stifled a yawn. The afternoon sun had almost lulled her into a nap, a luxury she would have scarcely thought possible weeks ago. 'I am surprised to hear he has posted a new development to us so soon.'

He lifted his brow at her as he came into the room.

'It has been over a week. I was surprised he had not had news sent to us earlier.'

A week? She quirked her lips.

'Has it already been a week since his last missive?' she asked. Days were tumbling one over another since she had arrived, and she and Ewan had fallen into a soft, gentle rhythm with one another. They spent time each day together and other times apart working on their own pursuits and activities. He settled in beside her, and the settee sank as it gave in to his weight. At first, she might have shuddered and been afraid of the man's proximity, but no more. She had grown to care for the ease he made her feel. He accepted her, and the kindness that she had viewed as weakness upon their first meeting, she now saw as the greatest strength a man could possess.

Butterflies whirled in her stomach as he smiled at her, his dimple flashing its usual warning that she needed to keep her feelings in check. Who knew what that letter held? Who knew what would happen at the end of their fortnight together? And heaven only knew how she would recover if he chose to move on without her.

'Care to do the honours, my lady?' he asked, extending the letter to her.

'Of course,' she answered with a bravado and confidence she did not feel. As she slid her finger under the wax seal, she prayed the news would be what she wanted. Too bad she didn't exactly know what she wanted that news to be.

While she knew she no longer wished to be Mrs Gordon, did she want to already be Lady Stewart? Did she want her freedom after all? Was she beginning to care far too much for this man she was not contractually allowed to love even if they did marry?

Her mind whirled with these questions, but she clamped them down as she flipped open the folded pages. She cleared her throat and read the correspondence aloud:

Laird Stewart,
After much exploration into the legality of your arrangement with Mr Gordon, and following up with the local laws, I have found that the exchange of money—your guinea—for Mr Gordon's property or goods—his wife—was legal, but that Mr Gordon was still viewed by the court of law as her husband.

After learning this, I attempted to locate Mr Gordon to speak with him about the terms of a legal divorce. After several days of seeking him and being unsuccessful, I visited the morgue on the suggestion of a local shopkeeper. Unfortunately, Mr Gordon was there. He had been brought in dead two days prior. Evidently he was killed by the husband of a woman he was found with. The man is now in custody and awaiting a hearing.

Due to Mr Gordon's unfortunate demise, Mrs Gordon is now a widow. The law does not recognize you as married to her based on your single agreement/transaction with Mr Gordon in the

*market. If you do wish to marry, you will have to
apply for a licence as one normally would.*

*If you have any further enquiries on the matter,
do let me know. This has been a very compelling
and unique case that has intrigued me. I appreciate, as always, your trust in me as your solicitor.*

*Sincerely,
James R. Sullivan*

*Dead?
Saints be.*

Catriona put down the letter and sat silently, taking in
the reality of what she had just read. She was free. But
free because Thomas was dead. Odd emotions welled
up in her. Happiness at her freedom, but also sadness
as to his gruesome murder, even if he had been a horrid man and husband.

But as of this very moment, she was no one's wife
and under no one's thumb. No more Thomas Gordon
harming her and blustering her about. No more harm
would come to her person, for she'd never allow it again.
The woman who had left Edinburgh was dead along
with Thomas. She was no longer his wife, nor would
she ever be. She choked on a sob as the emotion and
knowing of that shook her to her core.

She covered her mouth as she sobbed once more, her
eyes welling with tears, betraying her efforts to keep
her emotion at bay.

'I am sorry about Thomas,' Ewan offered. 'I know he
was your husband, despite—' he paused '—all he did.

I understand if this comes as a shock. Perhaps I should have read it on my own first.'

'Nay. I am sad for his brutal death, but these are tears of happiness and relief, for I am his wife no longer.'

Ewan cupped her face in his hand and gave a tentative smile. 'So, you are happy?'

'As horrible as it sounds to hear of another man's death. Aye. I am. I am free.'

'You *are* finally free. And you are safe.'

'Thank you,' she choked out, pressing a hand over his. As he wiped away one of her tears, she pulled him into a tight hug, unable to keep her happiness and gratitude at bay. 'You said you would save me, and you did. Thank you. Thank you for keeping your word to me. No one else other than Nettie ever has.'

Blazes.

He sucked in a breath. His whole body shuddered as she pressed against him. How long had he wished to hold her like this? She was warm and soft, and she smelled of summer. He sighed as he held her, closed his eyes, and stroked her hair as she wept on his shoulder. How much she had endured, he didn't know, and the imaginings of what such could have been clogged his throat. To know that she no longer hurt and was free from Mr Gordon filled Ewan's heart with hope even as it filled with dread. He could lose her now. Her decision to stay was in her hands as he had wanted it to be, but he'd never thought or dared imagine he would grow to care for her as much as he did now. He knew he wanted her here as Lady Stewart, even if he risked his heart by falling in love with her. Hell, whom was he fooling? Despite his best efforts, he already was falling for her slowly over the tiny little moments with her that breached his barriers each day.

She hiccupped against his neck, her lips skimming along his flesh there by accident and sending a thrill of alarm through him. He was a gentleman and disciplined in his affections, but if she continued to be so unintentionally alluring, it would be a struggle for him to remain so. Finally she leaned away from him and sat back against the cushion of the settee, wiping her eyes. Her whole face was as swollen and pink as a newborn baby squalling for milk, and yet she was gorgeous. He smiled at her.

'I am sorry, my laird.' She hiccupped again, still attempting to control her emotion. 'I had not realised how much I desired to be free of him and how bound up I was about what would come of that letter from your solicitor until I read it.' She shook her head. 'I am free.'

'Aye,' he answered in a croak of emotion. 'You are. And as we are nearly at the end of our fortnight arrangement with one another, you are free to make your choice. You may stay and be my wife, or you may leave to pursue your own future.'

Her eyes widened. 'You would not go back on your word?'

He scoffed. 'Nay. I made you a promise.' He reached out and took her hand between his own. 'While I would love for you to stay and be my wife as I think we suit one another well, I will set you free if that is your desire.'

Even if it breaks me in two.

'I thought you might change your mind now that the solicitor has sent his findings on to us.'

'If there is one thing I have learned through my own mistakes with Emogene as well as my father's mistakes in his attempts to arrange marriages for my sisters, it is that I want my wife to choose me as much as I choose her, and I do not want any woman to marry a man out of duty or desperation. No good came from those situations, and I will not repeat them.'

She said nothing but pulled her hand from his. 'I fear your touch clouds my judgement.' She smirked at him.

He laughed. 'You always surprise me, Catriona. It is one of the things I like best about you.'

'And I you.'

'So, what do you wish to do the rest of the afternoon before dinner?'

Her eyes lit like fire before she smiled and said, 'Ride.'

'You think you are ready to ride on your own? 'Tis only been over a week that you have worked with Hewe.'

'Aye. Hewe says I have a natural feel for riding, and I have already ridden alone. I just did not tell you.'

He grinned. 'Why am I not surprised? So, you are sure?'

She locked onto his gaze. 'I've never felt more ready for anything in all my life. I am finally free.'

Ewan couldn't believe the skill and nerve that Catriona had acquired over the week she had been working with the stable hands and Hewe to gain confidence in her horsemanship skills. She smiled with glee as Reed brought her preferred horse, a mare named Starlight, of all things. The first day she had ridden atop her, it had been a match, and Ewan wasn't surprised to see that Catriona had asked for them to saddle the beautiful brown mare with white markings along her nose.

'Ready?' he asked.

'Aye,' she answered. She mounted with ease and smiled at him. 'Race you to the large rowan tree at the end of the meadow,' she challenged him.

'What are we racing for?'

'Whatever it is you wish, my laird, although it doesn't matter. I shall win.' She urged her mare on with a click of her tongue and her boot.

Ewan laughed, and he and Wee Bit gave chase through the meadow. The horses galloped abreast, trimming the distance between the barn and designated rowan tree with speed. Catriona shouted and laughed as she rode, a joy he had never witnessed emanating from her. She was alive and happy, and all at once, Ewan realised he felt the same way. A wave of hope washed over him along with a desperate longing that she would choose him and Glenhaven and be a part of their lives forever.

The horses cut through the meadow, their hooves thundering along the grass, kicking up dirt. The ride and the sweet smell of the field filled his senses. There was nothing like galloping full out with the sun kissing your face and wind hitting your cheeks, washing away every care. So he gave in to the moment and forgot about all his worries as he revelled in Catriona's beauty, in being alive, and in being here as Laird of Glenhaven.

There was nowhere else he wished to be and no one else he wished to be with. He was content in who he was with her right now. The rowan tree became larger as they approached, and the two of them raced past its mighty limbs side by side. They pulled up to a slow cantor, and then into a walk, their horses breathing as heavily as they were.

'Seems another tie, my lady,' Ewan offered.

She laughed. 'Is there any other way for us to compete? Perhaps we do not wish the other to win but also do not wish to lose.'

'I think you may be on to something,' he added. He dismounted and led Wee Bit over to the shade of the tree where the horse could graze. He tossed the reins loosely over the lowest branch and walked over to assist Catriona with her dismount.

She accepted his hand and was easily guided down to the ground. His breath hitched at the sight of her. Colour was high in her cheeks from the exertion, her hair loose from its plait from the wind. The relaxed ease of her face made him literally weak in the knees, and his fingers tingled.

'You were right,' she murmured. 'Riding like that gives me a glorious sense of freedom. I am glad you encouraged me to get over my worries and try riding. I can with certainty tell you that I do indeed like it… as I do you.'

He stepped closer. 'You do?'

She batted his arm. 'As you well know.'

'Aye, I do know. And I have developed…affection for you…as you well know.' He was careful to not say *love*, for love was still forbidden to him. But affection and desire were allowed, and both burned brightly in him. He stepped closer to her, as close as possible without touching her. He'd been disciplined at keeping himself at bay as she was still officially married, but now…now that he knew she was no longer the wife of Mr Gordon, he found it even harder to stay the course.

She let her fingertips trail along the side of his face, and he summoned all the strength he had left not to react.

'So, what are we to do about it? 'Tis your decision as to whether you stay or go. All the cards of the future are in your hands to choose from. What say you?' he asked.

He held his breath for her answer.

'I cannot make such a decision without knowing one thing.'

'And what is that?'

'What it feels like for you to kiss me,' she murmured, moving closer.

He closed the space between them with one step and clutched her face, seizing her lips with the hunger and desire he had kept smouldering for so long. She matched the intensity of his kiss, which only heightened his pleasure. She wound her fingertips around the nape of his neck, and he deepened the kiss over and over. If he kissed her much longer, he'd be unable to pull away. The woman had asked for a kiss, not a ravishing, so he commanded himself to stop. With reluctance, he did just that.

As he stared into her eyes, her lips swollen and parted, the desire he saw there reflected his own. They were more than compatible, it seemed, on all accounts. It was up to her as to whether they had a life together, and for once he hated his own gallantry. Why had he offered her such an out?

Because he would not be like all the others in her life. He would not control her but give her a choice and voice in her future.

He clenched his jaw.

'You provide a persuasive argument, my laird. Those lips could bring a woman to swoon.'

He ran a thumb across her lips, his hunger for her still coursing through him.

She stilled his hand with her own. 'My answer is yes.'

Time stood still.

'Yes? Yes, to being my wife?'

'Aye, my laird. Despite my ability to choose freedom, I choose you, for you have taught me that I can have both.'

He seized her lips again and kissed her over and over and over.

Chapter Eighteen

'I cannot help but think upon the fact that meeting you was a miracle. All because I needed to go to the milliner's store. What are the odds?' Brenna said as she held up one square of fabric after another next to Catriona's cheek, while standing near the bank of windows in Catriona's room. 'Nay,' Brenna muttered, making a sour face. 'This one has a yellow undertone, which makes your beautifully creamy skin look quite ghastly.'

Catriona laughed. 'I have never received a finer compliment. Thank you, my lady,' she mocked, bobbing a faux curtsey at her soon-to-be sister-in-law. 'Are you sure they are not all the same shade? They all seem... blue.'

Brenna frowned. 'They are not all merely blue. Some have yellow undertones and others green. There are times when you sound just like Moira. My eldest sister will adore you.' She grinned. 'But only half as much as I do.'

'How can you adore me? You have only known me for two and a half weeks,' Catriona challenged her, part in jest but also part in truth. Why this family had accepted her so readily, she didn't understand. She'd not had a family for so long that she didn't trust the idea of having one again, despite how much love she felt for them already. More than she could ever have asked for. Although she'd have to be careful about her 'love' for Ewan. He was still bent on them not getting too caught up in feelings for one another.

Brenna set aside the squares of fabric and gripped Catriona by the shoulders. 'You are one of the most interesting women I have ever met. You are strong, have your own mind, and you…' Her eyes grew glassy with unshed tears, and she cleared her throat before continuing. 'And you have made my brother happy, which was something I did not dare dream possible.'

To her surprise, Catriona's own eyes filled with emotion. 'I hope I do not disappoint you,' she murmured before pulling Brenna into a hug.

'Never, sister. Never.'

'Never?'

Brenna stepped back. 'Not unless you do choose that ghastly blue fabric for your gown at our celebration ball next week to announce your engagement to Ewan.'

Catriona laughed. 'Speaking of the ball, what are my chances of the clan accepting me as Ewan's wife? I am a poor widow and not from the Highlands.'

'To be honest, they will all be against you from the start, but you will win them over just like you did us. You are a gem amongst women, Catriona. *We* are the ones lucky to have *you* in our lives. Now stay still as

I have a few more possibilities.' She held up another square and then tossed it aside with a flourish.

Catriona worried her hands, and her stomach flipped. She hoped dearly her future sister-in-law was right. Otherwise, this engagement of theirs might be very, very brief indeed.

Music from the main hall echoed throughout the walls of the salon at Glenhaven despite having the door closed. The evening of the ball had arrived in a blink, and here Catriona was about to be announced as the future Lady Stewart. She stared upon the portrait of the last Lady of Glenhaven and swallowed hard. Is this how she had felt upon the announcement of her marriage to Ewan's father? She doubted it. Self-confidence emanated from the woman's keen, unflinching gaze and subtle smirk.

'I wish you would tell me your secrets, my lady. I am in dire need of them.'

Catriona rubbed her arms from the chill of expectation and paced up and down the length of the room once more. She knew it was almost time for Ewan to fetch her for the announcement.

Was it too late to run?

She stilled. *Fool.* She didn't wish to run. She wanted to stay. The life she could have with Ewan and his family was more than she had ever dreamed possible for herself and her future, but nagging fear raced through her. What if they rejected her? Shamed her for having such a murky past? She'd already endured enough shame and hate for a lifetime and didn't wish to have any more rebukes thrust upon her, especially by those who didn't know her.

The door squeaked open, and Catriona turned from where she stood in the shadows of the room.

'You could not look more lovely,' Ewan murmured, his voice husky and deep as he closed the door behind him.

Appreciation glowed in his gaze as his eyes swept over her. Warmth and happiness loosened the knot in her chest. No man had ever looked at her with such reverence as if she were beauty itself and he a mere pauper allowed to gaze upon her. She fidgeted with the locket around her neck. It hung at her throat on a matching blue ribbon from Brenna. That way she could wear it nestled around her neck rather than hidden deep in her bodice.

Catriona sighed at the sight of him upon approach. 'And *you*, Laird Stewart, will make every woman at this ball weak in the knees at the sight of you.' She meant it. Even now, a quiver ran up her arm as he stood before her with his blue-green eyes piercing into her and dressed in his regal red Stewart plaid, which revealed his muscular knees and calves. He wore his finest white tunic and cravat, and a black dress coat. Even his dark hair had been styled with care, not a single strand out of place.

He looked every bit a laird.

And she was a no one.

She swallowed hard as doubt thrust itself between the two of them.

He pressed a kiss to her cheek and meandered towards her lips, eventually capturing them for a heated and full kiss, which melted all her doubt and reason away.

'You make thinking clearly quite a challenge, my laird,' she murmured after he pulled back. He smelled of tallow and mint, and she breathed him in as he ran both his hands down her bare arms, sending her senses ablaze.

'Are you ready for the wrath that shall consume you upon your announcement?' she asked, unable to keep her fears at bay after all. Her nerves were frayed and taut at the knowing that the excitement over their news would most likely send the clan and its leaders into uncertainty and chaos.

'The elders loved you when they came to dine,' he offered.

'Aye. They loved Mrs Gordon, cousin to Laird Mac-Lean, who had no intention of staying. When they learn the truth about my past and that I will be part of the clan and their future as Lady Stewart, I believe their love of me shall morph into something quite different. Something more akin to hate.'

She was relieved to have at least said it aloud, so she did not have to hold all her worries upon her heart alone. That was what marriage would be, would it not? A sharing of concerns and bearing the weight of burdens equally, as well as events that gave cause for celebration?

He leaned his forehead against hers. 'They may be upset or even angry, but that will not deter me or my decision. I hope it will not change yours.'

'Not a chance,' she said with as much courage as she could muster. Truth be told, she wasn't sure. She was nervous and had a pit of worry settled deep in her stomach, where her doubts lingered and multiplied. Over the years, she'd learned not to trust the possibility of good things.

She also wanted to be able to tell the man she loved the truth, that she was indeed falling for him and longed for their marriage to be allowed the complication of love, but the man didn't wish to be loved, did he? So she shoved it down deep with her doubt about being accepted and gifted the laird a smile instead.

'Shall we go?' he asked. 'While the music and spirits are high? Mrs Stevens tells me everyone has arrived, even the elders.'

'I suppose I cannot hide out in here all night. The clarsach and I have not quite come to an understanding yet, as you well know.'

He offered his arm to her, which she readily accepted. 'There will be time enough for more lessons, Mrs Gordon. I plan to teach you them all.'

She smiled.

He whispered in her ear. 'And many of those lessons will have nothing to do with music.'

His devilish smirk made her laugh, and before she knew it, she was within the hall by his side. The room glowed with candlelight and wealth. Ladies were adorned with jewels and the finest gowns, and the men wore their best plaid, jackets, and broaches. Shoes shone from a recent polish, and the air was alive with the smells of cooked meats, sweet cakes, and wine. A more glorious celebration she could not have imagined. She met Brenna's gaze across the room and smiled. Her future sister-in-law nodded back, her face full of determination and happiness.

A hush filled the room at the sight of Ewan and Catriona together, and she lifted her chin and steadied herself. If nothing else, she needed to look like a lady even if she didn't entirely feel like one in her bones. But she knew if she looked weak or uncertain about herself, people would crush her to the ground. So she smiled, squared her shoulders, and remembered that he had chosen her, he had saved her, and she owed him more than she could ever repay. She'd not embarrass him or herself. She would act like Lady Stewart, and anyone who besmirched her also besmirched him. And she'd not let that happen. He had given her an opportunity for a new life, a different life far beyond what she could have ever dreamed possible for herself. She'd not let anyone seize it from her now that she had also chosen it.

'Ladies and gentlemen,' Ewan began, his voice booming across the crowd of guests, 'thank you for coming this eve to celebrate my upcoming nuptials with my bride, whom I will introduce to you now: Catriona Gordon from Edinburgh.'

Since she couldn't claim a home to be from, they had decided upon Edinburgh. Anyone who dug much further into it would know quickly that she had been raised in Lismore and had no living relatives. She held her smile as all of this raced through her mind and a silence fell over the crowd. When the quiet extended to one beat and then another, Laird MacLean raised his tankard. 'Slainte!'

Despite a bit of an awkward pause, the crowd echoed

his cheers to them and drank from their cups. Then, thankfully the music started up again. Ewan kissed her cheek, grabbed her hand, and guided them through the throngs of people to Laird MacLean and Brenna. Slowly the noise in the room picked up as the guests returned to dancing, chatting, and feasting.

'Saving the day as always. Thank you, brother,' said Ewan, clapping Laird MacLean on the shoulder.

'Just helping out a fellow laird,' he joked. 'Congratulations to the happy couple-to-be,' he said.

'Thank you,' Catriona answered. 'For allowing me to claim you as family, and for bringing that rather awkward silence to an end.'

'You will be family soon, and I am grateful for such an honour,' he replied. 'Now, just be yourself, and they will adore you.'

His kindness helped to calm the worry racing through her. She would do just as he said and circulate about the crowd to meet as many people as she could; she would not cower and hide as if she should be ashamed. Her past was just that and nothing she could control. Her future as Lady Stewart started now.

'Perhaps I will do just that, my laird,' she replied, lifting a brow at him.

'Not alone you won't,' Brenna added. 'Allow me to help you weave through the lion's and lioness's dens.' She flashed Catriona an impish smile and wove her arm through hers, and off into the crowd they went.

They greeted several of what Brenna described as the more powerful women of the clan, as their husbands had been advisors to her late father. Some of them were kind, while others endured an exchange of pleasantries but little more.

'I cannot help but notice the elders have made their way to Ewan. Shall we rescue him?' Catriona asked as she watched halfway across the room.

Brenna studied him and shook her head. 'Nay. He is handling his own. Garrick is also with him. Despite his innate kindness, he can cut a man down to the quick if need be.' She leaned closer. 'Besides, you must meet Susanna Cameron, whose brother is laird. The Camerons are the most powerful clan in the Highlands, especially since the fall of the Campbells, who had quite a battle with their long-time rivals, the MacDonalds. Rumour has it that it was Susanna and her men who helped Laird Campbell rescue his now wife and child from being murdered at the hands of her own father.'

'What?' Catriona asked stopping in her tracks. 'Can you explain that again?'

'No matter for now.' She waved her hand. 'Come. You will adore her, I promise. Her glare can slay a man, I tell you.' She sighed. 'If only I had such powers.'

Catriona smiled and followed behind Brenna as the men and women were packed in tightly on this side of the banquet hall.

'Why are there so many soldiers over here?' Catriona muttered as she passed by dozens of them chatting with their tankards of ale and wine. One almost sloshed his drink on her as she squeezed by. 'And some appear rather deep in their cups,' she added, glancing back at a soldier who almost fell over his own boots.

'No need to worry. The Camerons always travel with soldiers, many soldiers.'

'All of these soldiers are watching over this one woman?' she asked.

'Aye. Her brothers were unable to attend, so these men are also her escorts to ensure her safety.'

When she reached Brenna's side, Catriona paused and met the gaze of a woman whose eyes seemed capable of cutting through stone. They were a light ice blue in stark contrast to her pitch-black hair and pale, pearly skin. Despite being indoors, she was partially hidden by the hood of her dark cloak, and Brenna could only imagine how shockingly beautiful she might be without hiding part of herself from the world.

'Susanna,' Brenna began, 'this is Catriona Gordon, my future sister-in-law. And Catriona, this is Susanna Cameron, sister of Laird Cameron. We share a border with her people.'

'Lovely to meet you, Miss Cameron,' Catriona offered up, unable to look away from the woman's compelling gaze.

Susanna paused and stepped closer. 'Have we met before, Miss Gordon?' she asked, her gaze falling to the locket around Catriona's neck.

She fought the urge to take a step back and commanded herself to hold her ground. According to Brenna, this woman and her clan were important, and Catriona needed to make a good impression on her. 'Nay, my lady. Prior to a few weeks ago, I did not often travel up to the Highlands from Edinburgh.'

She commended herself on how calm she sounded as

she wove an answer that resembled truth even though one couldn't say it was completely true. Brenna glanced over at her and cleared her throat.

'You are sure?'

Catriona searched her memory, and nothing came up. 'If you do not mind me saying, Miss Cameron, I do not believe I would have forgotten such a meeting. You have a very distinctive face and compelling presence about you.'

The woman's gaze shifted to Catriona's face, and she smiled and nodded. 'You are correct in that not many people forget me. But you also have a remarkable face, and your eyes, such an unusual shade of gold and brown.'

'Thank you,' Catriona answered. A small seed of uncertainty budded within her. Just as she had always been able to sense when Thomas was in a foul temper, Catriona could feel something was in the air with Miss Cameron. Catriona's throat tightened as she prepared for whatever verbal lashing the woman was about to give her.

'And where did you come by that locket?'

Catriona's pulse increased, her heart pounding in her chest as if she were riding in the fields on Starlight's back. 'I do not know, but I have always had it. For as long as I can remember,' she answered, her throat suddenly dry.

'Oh?' Susanna asked taking another half step towards her. 'You have no recollection at all?' Her tone was sharp and unyielding. She gripped Catriona's upper arm.

'I don't understand what I've said to upset you, Miss

Cameron. I honestly do not know who gave me the locket.'

The woman tightened her grip, and a wildness came into her blue eyes. A few soldiers noted her distress and closed ranks around them. Brenna chimed in as she was pressed close to Catriona. 'Susanna? What is this all about? Tell your men to stand down.'

'I will do no such thing until this woman tells me who she is and how she came by this locket.' Susanna glared at her, pain flashing bright in her eyes.

'I am Catriona Gordon from Edinburgh.'

'I know what you have said, but I doubt the truth of your words,' she hissed in frustration. 'Who gave you this locket?' She yanked Catriona close to her face.

Alarmed, Catriona tried to pull back from her, but it was too late. The circle around them was too tight, and Susanna's grip far too strong. There was nowhere to go. Against her better judgement, she stated the truth. 'I do not know. I cannot remember much before I was around six years old.'

'And why not?'

'Because I lost my family at sea. I woke on the shoreline with no memory of who I was or where I was from. I was lucky to have survived and been found by Nettie, a woman who then raised me.'

'You believe yourself to be an orphan?' The woman gasped.

'Aye, my lady,' she said, shame heating her cheeks. 'I don't just believe it. I am one. I have no family.'

Chapter Nineteen

Susanna let go of Catriona's arm as if the words she spoke slapped her. Catriona rubbed her upper arm where the woman had gripped her so fiercely.

'That's not possible…' Susanna began, but paused, noting that a crowd had gathered and that many of the conversations around them had ceased as others watched their exchange. 'Not here,' she commanded and clutched Catriona by the wrist.

Frightened and confused by the woman's bizarre behaviour, Catriona freed herself. 'Nay,' she said as calmly as she could without creating a greater scene. 'I'll not go anywhere with you, Miss Cameron, until I know what this is about.'

Susanna dropped her voice low. 'Trust me in that you do not want this conversation aired about in here for everyone to hear.' Her eyes flashed with a warning Catriona decided to heed.

'Then I will find Laird Stewart and meet you and your men in the salon, but I will not be dragged from here by force.' She'd been treated so before, but she'd promised herself never again. And that meant today. It didn't matter if Miss Cameron was from the most influential clan in the Highlands. She only hoped Ewan would understand and that she didn't muck up too much by standing up for herself.

Susanna nodded, which seemed the closest Catriona would get to a verbal agreement, so she began scanning the room for Ewan. Brenna was at her side as she carved a path through the crowd.

'What happened?' Brenna asked. 'I've never seen her like that before. She's usually as composed and cool as a frozen loch, but not today.'

'I don't know. None of it made any sense, but she seemed quite undone by my locket. Why?' she mused. 'It is a rather crude piece of jewellery worn by time and age. I only cherish it as it is from my childhood. I do not even know who gifted it to me. Nettie said I had it on me the day she found me.'

'That is odd. Why would Susanna care a whit about your locket or who gave it to you?'

'That is exactly what we must find out, but I need Ewan to be there in case things go poorly. If she is as important as you say, this situation between us could have a devastating effect on the clan, and I don't wish for that at all. Will you help me find him?'

'Aye,' Brenna murmured. 'Him and Garrick.'

Catriona and Brenna continued, struggling to see over the heads of tall soldiers and around the billowing gowns of the ladies in attendance, as they made their way through the crowd.

'Ah!' Brenna cried out. 'I see them. Their backs were

to us, which is why they did not see the exchange and come to intercede. I will let them know what has happened. We will meet you in the salon.'

She paused. What if she went in there and he didn't come? What if he saw it as a sign that she had failed in her duties as Lady Stewart before she had even begun?

Trust him.

If she wanted to marry this man, which she did, she had to start trusting him. Right now. Not when it was easy, but when it was hard. She snaked through the crowd as quickly as she dared without drawing any more undue attention to herself and made her way into the salon. She closed the door behind her and stared up at the portrait of Lady Stewart.

Why did I ever think I could do this? I've already upset the most prominent clan in the Highlands as well as the elders, and my engagement to your son has only just been announced. What do I do now?

She would do what she always did.

She sucked in a deep breath and released it, not once but twice. Then she squared her shoulders, lifted her chin, and carried on.

The door opened behind her. Ewan and Brenna rushed in with Garrick not far behind.

'What is this Brenna tells me about Susanna Cameron?' Ewan asked, his brow furrowed. He reached Catriona and took her hands in his own.

She met his gaze, her nerves settled by his words and his touch. There was no anger, only concern for her in his tone. Why had she been so worried? Her stomach fluttered in relief. 'She was certain we had met before, but I told her we hadn't. Then she carried on about this locket, which has no value to anyone but me.'

'Your locket?' he asked.

'Aye.'

'Why?'

'I don't know, but when I could not answer who gifted it to me, she became more upset. Finally she asked for us to speak outside of the hall, to not draw any further attention to our conversation. She was becoming quite…impassioned by it all, and people were starting to notice. There were more than a few gazes set upon us as we spoke.' She gripped Ewan's hand, steadied by the warm, firm pressure of his hold. 'I fear I may have embarrassed you already. I confessed to her I was an orphan to try to convince her and calm her that she was mistaken in her thoughts as to who I was.' She searched his gaze seeing if this would be what drove him off, but he kissed her hand instead.

'You could never embarrass me. I'm glad you told her the truth. Now people will know just how strong you are, like I do.'

Her breath caught in her throat. Before she could reply, the door opened. Susanna Cameron strode in with her long, dark cloak trailing behind her, along with three of her men. She nodded, and they closed the door and stood guarding it, providing them the privacy and perhaps the barricade she asked for.

'My laird,' she said as she saw Ewan. 'Thank you for joining us.'

Ewan let go of Catriona's hands and stepped between her and Susanna. 'You seem to have made a scene, Miss

Cameron. Care to explain why you are harassing my betrothed on the night of our celebration? Surely your enquiry can wait.' His words held a chastisement to her behaviour that couldn't be missed. He sounded like a laird setting a member of his community in their place, and Catriona commanded herself to keep her mouth closed. This Ewan she had never seen before.

Susanna paused and after a moment backed down. 'You are right. My apologies, my laird. I regret that I could not better control my emotions at the sight of her. It was a shock.' The woman looked past him to Catriona, and the sentiment in her eyes was unmistakable. Was it grief? Sadness?

Catriona could make no sense of it all.

Ewan shook his head. 'Miss Cameron, you are speaking in riddles, and I grow impatient. There is much to attend to this eve, and I would like to celebrate with my bride-to-be. Why are we here, and what is it you want?' A dark edge gave his words an added warning.

Susanna's ice-blue eyes flashed up to match his challenge. 'Surely you remember the summer of 1726, my laird.'

'What?' he asked, his brow crinkled.

'We are about the same age, if I remember correctly, so we both would have been almost ten years old.' Her eyes filled with emotion. 'Catriona would have been about six at that time.'

Ewan stilled; his body tensed. He held Susanna's gaze and then turned to Catriona as if seeing her for the first time. 'Susanna,' he whispered, his voice husky. 'It cannot be.'

'I believe it is.'

'But all this time…' Ewan covered his mouth with his hand and shook his head.

Catriona looked to both of them. 'I do not understand either of you. Brenna, can you explain this to me?'

Brenna's mouth was gaping open. 'The Lost Girl,' she murmured. 'Moira and I never wanted to swim along the loch after that summer for fear of—' She stopped.

Blast. Everyone was speaking in puzzles that she could not decipher. 'For fear of what, Brenna?' Catriona asked, her heart raging in her chest.

'Being lost at sea,' Ewan answered as he took her hand in his. 'The Camerons' youngest daughter disappeared at the beach near Loch Linnhe the summer of 1726, pulled out to sea in the undertow. Word of her disappearance spread to all the clans in the area. We spent months looking for any sign of her. When she was never found, she was believed to be dead.' He shook his head. 'You told us of your memory of being at the beach and being lost at sea, and Nettie's belief that your family had died at sea when your boat must have capsized, but I did not even consider you might have been the lost Cameron sister. I should have thought of it, but I didn't. It was so long ago.'

Catriona stared back at them in disbelief.

'I believe you are my long-lost younger sister, Violet,' said Susanna.

'You believe I am your sister? Why? It has been so long. How—' Catriona sputtered, and then stopped just as abruptly as she became overwhelmed by the assertion.

A smile softened the woman's features and made her even more beautiful. 'It was your eyes at first. My sister always had the most stunning amber-gold eyes, much like yours. And then when I saw the locket about your neck, I nearly fell to my knees. It is the locket I gave my sister before she disappeared.' Her eyes welled, but she blinked back the tears.

No doubt Susanna Cameron was not a woman who cried in public.

Catriona felt numb. Her toes and fingers tingled, and a strange feeling of floating came over her. How could any of what she was saying be true? Was this woman merely mad with grief because Catriona resembled a sister she had lost?

'What you are saying would be most remarkable if it were true,' Laird MacLean offered. 'It would mean she would be a part of the Cameron clan, a sister of the laird, like you.' He came closer to Miss Cameron. 'Is there some way that you could prove what you say may be true other than your memories of her?'

'Does your locket still have the tiny, pressed violet I put in it all of those years ago for your birthday?' she asked, a wistfulness in her voice.

Catriona opened the locket. 'Nay,' she answered, shifting on her feet. 'I am sorry. It contains nothing. It never has. It is empty.'

Susanna's eyes closed and she shook her head. 'If only my brothers were here. I know Rolf and Royce would be able to say for certain. They would be able to confirm or deny my claim.'

'But they are not here, my lady,' Ewan stated. 'While

it is *possible* she may be your sister, there is also every possibility she is not. I know you wish for her to be your sister, but the chances…'

Susanna sighed. 'I know the chances are small, especially after all these years, but there is still a chance. Could you come to us, to our home at Loch's End, so we could talk?' Susanna pleaded. 'Perhaps being there or speaking with my brothers will spark a memory.'

Catriona met the woman's desperate gaze. She didn't know if she wished for it to be true or not. Could it be that she wasn't an orphan? That she had a family? That all this time, she had just been lost to them?

That she could have lived an altogether different life, a better one?

Her stomach dropped, and she felt ill. She clutched Ewan's arm for support. Susanna rushed to her, but Catriona pushed her away.

'Get away from me,' Catriona shouted through her anguish, her voice sounding nothing like her own. 'I do not know you. And even if you were my family, why did you not search for me to the ends of the earth rather than abandoning me? Why?'

Susanna staggered back, her face pained and uncertain as her soldiers rushed to her sides to steady her. 'You do not understand, sister,' she pleaded. 'We thought you dead.'

'You are just one of many that gave up on me, my lady,' she said, gripping Ewan's arm. 'Please take me out of here, my laird.'

'Catriona,' he reasoned. 'If there is any chance that

she is indeed your sister, then you must speak with her. You cannot just run away…'

'My sister, my family, would not have given up on finding me. This is *not* my sister,' she stated, glaring at Susanna. 'I cannot be in this room a moment longer.'

She shook off Ewan's hold and ran past all of them to the door. She moved quickly down the corridor, doing her best to keep the tears and hysteria that threatened at bay. Thankfully most of the guests were so deep in their cups or enthralled by dancing that few of them gave her any notice at all.

When she burst through the door to the outside, she ran down the hill until she reached her favourite spot: a large, flat shelf of a rock that acted as a bench for her to sit upon. She gathered her gown into a bundle and hoisted herself up on the stone. She sat and sighed as she leaned back on the cool, hard surface. The pressure soothed the ache in her chest, and the sight of the stars in the night sky helped her heart regain a more regular rhythm.

Only the heavens seemed to understand her. Other than Ewan. She smiled at the thought of his kindness, his smile, and his support. She knew he had not meant anything unkind in his suggestion to stay and speak to Susanna, but he did not understand. How could he? He'd had a family all his life. Even if they'd been difficult and he'd suffered loss, he'd known them and knew who he was and where he belonged. He was the son of a laird and a Stewart, and he always had been.

But her?

She'd been lost to the world with singular snippets

of memory to tether her to her past and what had been her family. If Susanna's supposition was true, then Catriona was a Cameron, one of the most prominent clans in the Highlands, and she was the sister of the laird. Tears streamed down her cheeks, and she released the sobs she'd held at bay. She wept until she could cry no more. She wept for the life that could have been. For the life lost to the sea.

Chapter Twenty

'How is Catriona?' Brenna asked from the doorway of Ewan's study.

He set aside the map he'd been poring over with little progress. 'As horrid as you might imagine. She refuses to let anyone in her chamber except for Betsy.'

Brenna scoffed. 'Ewan, has it escaped you that not only is she your betrothed, but that you are the laird, own this castle, and can make a demand to see her?'

Ewan frowned. 'I don't think that would be well-received. If anything, that would make things entirely worse, for she would be angry with me.'

'Angry at you for checking on her? Caring for her? That is no crime.' She sifted through some of the piles on his desk, and he playfully slapped her hand away.

'Do you have nothing to entertain yourself with today?' he asked. 'If not, I have many a letter you could draft for me.'

She lifted her brow at him. 'Well, I could do that for you if you would do something for me by checking on your soon-to-be wife?' She sent him a sweet smile.

He sighed. 'You will grant me no peace until I do this, will you?'

'Nay. I will not, brother.'

'Fine,' he murmured. He stood, gathered a pile of correspondence, a stack of fresh parchment, and his ink pot and quill, and set them before her on the large table. 'If you will be so kind as to deal with this, I will speak with her. Let us hope we are both productive in our endeavours.'

'Be sure to straighten your cravat, brother,' she called after him. 'You look like the devil.'

The last thing he cared about today was his appearance. Two days had passed since the celebration, and Catriona had barely left her chambers. And he wouldn't be his father and demand an audience with her. He could, however, insist she speak with him to ensure her well-being. Those two things were different, weren't they?

He frowned. Not really.

Soon he was at her chamber door, so whether they were different or not didn't matter. He was already here. He knocked loudly. When no one answered, he knocked again. 'Catriona? I must speak with you. I need to know you are well. I have not seen you for days.'

'I am well, my laird.'

'May I speak with you, so I can see with my own eyes? I miss you.' The last three words slipped out. Why the devil had he said that? He cringed.

No romantic entanglements, remember?

He was on a slippery slope. He didn't wish to mess up the fine arrangement they had now by loving his future wife. That would only lead to heartache and ruin. He was certain of it.

After a long pause, he heard footsteps, and then the lock on the door clicked. She didn't open the door for him, but offered, 'You may come in.'

He opened the door to find the room neat as a pin and glimmering with sheen. 'Have you been cleaning?' he asked, unable to suppress his curiosity.

'When I am upset, I clean. Is that a problem, my laird? I have already made Betsy cross with me about it. Shall I add you to the list?'

He clenched his jaw. *Deuces.* She was in a fine temper. Why did he ever listen to Brenna? Catriona was in no mood to speak to anyone, let alone him.

Each question she asked was a skilfully laced trap, and he was sure to misstep and land himself in a load of horse dung fit to drown a man. He ran a hand through his hair.

'Well?' she prodded. 'You have seen me. I am well. Is there anything else?' She set a glare on him that would have made his mother proud. He stilled like a deer.

There was no right answer, and he knew it, so he forged on with a truth he would have wanted someone to share with him. He approached her and placed a hand on her arm. She flinched under his touch but did not move away.

'You cannot ignore the issue forever,' he said. 'Why will you not just visit the Camerons? It will help you find out the truth one way or the other. And the answer does not even matter. Either way, we will marry and live our lives, but at least you will know. It will no longer be a question mark in your life.'

She scoffed and moved out of his reach. 'It will not matter? You must be teasing me. There is no winning. If they are my long-lost family, I will know what all I have lost. If they are not, then my hopes will be dashed. Either choice is heartbreak. Can you not see that?' she said, her eyes sparking with emotion.

Bollocks. He saw that now. 'I did not think of it that way, but you're right. I don't know how you feel because I have not lived your life. But I want to help you. To be your partner in this. To try to do what a husband would and support you,' he said, squeezing the bridge of his nose. 'Even if I make a terrible muck of it while trying.'

'Why will no one leave me to make up my own mind on things?' she replied and walked right past him and out through the door, muttering as she walked down the corridor.

'Mrs Gordon?' Betsy called. Ewan turned to find her standing in the hallway with fresh linens, staring after Catriona.

'I came to speak with her,' Ewan offered.

'Aye. How did it go, my laird?' she asked, clutching the linens to her chest.

'Not as well as I had hoped, Betsy.'

'Best give her some time to cool off, my laird. She's not been herself since the ball.'

'Aye. She hasn't. Perhaps some fresh air will do her some good.'

He'd give her time for her temper to cool and seek her out once more. He knew that anything worth having was worth fighting for, and above all things, he'd fight for her whether she wanted him to or not.

'I thought I might find you here,' said Ewan as he reached the top of the slope overlooking the loch below.

Hours had passed since he'd tried to speak with her. He'd even dined without her, but he wouldn't be able to sleep until he'd spoken to her, even if she didn't wish to speak to him.

Catriona faced him, and Ewan's steps faltered. The glow of the sunset cast a golden radiance about her skin, setting her amber eyes and auburn crown ablaze as a few wisps of hair flitted about her face in the light breeze. Despite having been with her for weeks now, the sheer beauty of her continued to arrest and steal his senses in the best and most complete of ways. And she was to be his wife.

'Oh?' she said.

'Aye,' he answered, smiling and closing the few steps remaining between them. He nodded to the wolfhound charging up the hill towards them. 'Whenever I cannot find Rufus, I know you are here with him and he with you.'

Rufus trotted up to him and leaned into his thigh, his pink tongue lolling out of the side of his mouth as he panted.

'Traitor,' Ewan murmured, casting a playful narrowing gaze at his beloved dog, who pressed against him to accept a scratch behind the ear.

'He is a dear companion,' she added, smiling at Rufus. 'I never had a dog before, and I find I might like to have a pack of them. They are fine company. They listen, but offer no advice, which works well for me.' She lifted her brows meaningfully at Ewan, crossed her arms against her chest, and faced the loch and the orange-pink sky.

Ack. Just as he thought. He'd bungled their previous conversation. He should have just listened instead of attempting to solve anything. She'd found out that she might have a family thought long lost to her, a subject he knew nothing about. Rubbing the back of his neck, he stared out at the water. Perhaps he could tell her what he did know. He stilled and his hand dropped to his side.

Or he could just apologise. He shifted on his feet.

'I'm sorry.'

The words felt and sounded like he'd swallowed a fistful of pebbles.

Her form stiffened at his words. Perhaps she was as surprised as he.

When she didn't respond, he wondered if he'd said them at all.

'What for?' she said.

Ah, so he had said the words, and she had heard them. He tugged at his coat sleeve and came a step closer, allowing his shoulder to brush against her own.

'For being an arse. I should have listened to you rather than offered advice.'

He studied her profile as she stared out at the loch, its grey waters as still and smooth as glass despite the light puffs of breeze that ruffled the vibrant green grass along the glen. A bird flew off a tree branch, swooping low and then high. Rufus barked and charged off after it. She smiled. 'Such a simple life, I envy,' she whispered.

'Oh?' he replied. 'Why? It seems frustrating to chase prey one never catches.'

'It is that he is never deterred. Never gives up. Each day is a new start as if yesterday is forgotten. Each eve when we come out at dusk to walk, he charges headlong into this meadow and towards a loch that he has seen a thousand days as if he has never run the track of it before.'

'Such can be your life as well,' he said. 'You can choose joy and let every day be a fresh start and new beginning.'

'As could you,' she answered setting her gaze on him once more.

Her words landed like an arrow hitting its mark. 'You are right,' he murmured reluctantly. 'As terrifying as such a risk for hope might be.' He smiled. 'You have a keen way of turning my own words around on me.'

She chuckled. 'And you hate it, do you not?'

'I abhor it,' he answered, finding laughter tinging the ends of his words as well.

'Why?'

'It quite reminds me of my sister Moira.' He paused. 'And my mother, truth be told.'

'Walk with me. Perhaps you can tell me more about them both. Despite your complaints, I hear the warmth and affection in your voice. It will distract me from my anger at you,' she teased.

He offered his arm, and she accepted it as if they

had done it a thousand times before like Rufus charging along the meadow.

The unexpected feel of her body nestled up to his sent a feathering of desire and excitement along his limbs. His bicep flexed as he tugged her a mite closer, as close as he dared. 'A walk along the loch it is,' he answered, keen to not lose this moment. She'd not offered her touch since the ball, and he dared not lose his advantage. He was keen to win back her favour.

Rufus circled back, whipping past them, and Catriona laughed. The sound tightened his chest, but he spoke despite it. 'My mother and Moira had much in common. They even looked alike. Moira was like a smaller version of my mother, and as the eldest, she could run us about as she wished. I adore her, though. She is smart and clever and knows everything about anything with leaves.' He swallowed. 'And she is brave…and she is a survivor, much like you.' His chest tightened further. 'Mother was the same, which is why losing her was such a shock to all of us. In the blink of an eye, she was dead. I always argued with Moira that she had not died of a weakened heart, but that her heart had far too much love to hold. That when she'd died, all that love went free into the air, the soil, the trees, the birds…and into us. Mere foolish fancies, I know.'

'Nay. Perhaps it is true, and now all her love is around you. Always,' she whispered, meeting his gaze.

His throat constricted at the unexpected emotion coursing through him. His mother had been gone for so long, his reaction surprised him. And why in the world was he telling her all this? He'd never told anyone other than Moira.

Then the truth struck him like a lightning bolt, and his muscles seized.

He'd told her because he knew she understood him and his loss and felt it down to the ache in her soul. It sat reflected in her eyes and in the pulled-down corners of her mouth. Yet despite what it would stir in her, she still wanted to know everything, even if it pained her to walk through such loss because it reminded her of her own.

He couldn't speak, not trusting what would fall from his lips. They stopped and stood in silence, and she nestled further into his body, leaning her head on his shoulder.

Blazes.

Merely the feel of her set his body aflame, and he closed his eyes. He could never let her know the power she had over him or she would crush him, just like Emogene. And he would be left even smaller than he already was.

Or perhaps she wouldn't. She wasn't Emogene. What if she empowered him and made him the best version of himself, making him far greater than he could ever be without her by his side?

He wanted to believe in her, in them, in love…but could he trust it?

He should pull away, step out of their semblance of an embrace. She might soon become his wife, but he couldn't dare love her, could he?

He opened his eyes and shifted on his feet, garnering the courage to step out of their hold, when she spoke.

'At least you can remember her. I cannot remember my mother or father, no matter how hard I try. I squeeze my eyes shut willing just one blurry image of either of them, but nothing comes.'

'Nothing? You can remember nothing of them at all?'

The wind whipped up, and she shivered against him. 'Here,' he offered instinctively. He unbuttoned his overcoat with the intention of removing it and draping it over her shoulders, but she slid under the jacket with him, igniting a trail of fire against his tunic as she snuggled against his side, her arm resting around his waist.

He cleared his throat.

'Thank you. That is better,' she murmured, her voice reverberating through his body.

For her perhaps, but he was in agony. The smell, feel, and heat of her were lancing through his self-control after not seeing or feeling her for days, so he gave in and pulled her closer, his arm embracing her petite waist.

'At least I remember I had brothers and a sister, but I do not know if they were Susanna and her brothers. If I close my eyes, I can smell the salt of the sea air, the feel of the warm sun on my face, and hear their laughter as we chased one another towards the water before the wave crashed over me. They have been lost to me for so long that the possibility of them being alive and in my life now seems like a dream. One that is far too good to come true.'

'I cannot imagine how that feels. I am sorry, Catriona.'

'I know you are, and I am not angry at you, but the situation. You just happened to be there, offering me advice this afternoon that I did not want to hear, so I took my frustrations out on you. I am sorry, too.'

'So, what will you do? You know the Camerons are relentless. They will send you correspondence every day for the rest of our lives begging for you to visit, or they may very well appear on the drive, demanding entry to Glenhaven to speak with you.'

'You think so?' She sighed. 'I would have thought it would not have mattered after all of this time whether I was their sister or not.'

'Look at you. Who would not want you in their life? I know I am the greater man for it,' he offered and paused, turning her in his arms to face her.

'Really?' she asked, doubt in her eyes.

'Aye. You, Mrs Catriona Gordon, have helped me become a better man in the few weeks I have known you. Imagine what you will do for me over a lifetime.' He laughed and tucked a strand of hair behind her ear. 'You cannot begrudge their efforts to know the truth, can you?'

'Aye.' She sighed again. 'I suppose not. And I do wish to know. I am just fearful of how I will feel. Of what it will change in my life. I have had nothing until now. And then suddenly, I have options: I have you, and I have a possible long-lost family. It is more goodness than I can trust.'

'That is how I feel about you,' he replied.

'Ah, is that how you feel about being a laird as well? That it will all be taken from you in a moment?'

He stiffened. Such thoughts he tried to avoid these days. He had far too much to lose than he wanted to acknowledge. Self-doubt began to weave its imperceptible webs. His throat dried.

'You can tell me the truth. I will not tell anyone your doubts,' she said.

He released a breath and a chuckle all at once as unease and relief duelled within. 'Am I so easy to read?'

'You need not pretend with me. We will hold each other's secrets as husband and wife, will we not?' She lifted her face to him, her gaze searching his own for the truth.

Could he pretend and lie to her even if he dared? She would see right through him, would she not?

He nodded. 'I suppose we will, so aye, I have doubts. I am trying desperately to be the laird my father was and to guide our clan to prosperity rather than ruin, but...' He halted in exasperation.

She stepped out of his hold. 'But what?'

He ran a hand through his hair. 'But I do not want to become *him* in order to do that.'

'Who says you must? Can you not be a leader in your own right? You are Ewan Stewart, not Bran Stewart. Lead with kindness rather than an iron fist.'

He narrowed his gaze at her and crossed his arms against his chest. 'Be myself?'

'Aye,' she answered with lifted brow. 'As I've said before, who else can you be? Do you remember your lesson in the barn? It is only by trusting your instincts that you will be able to be the laird I know you can and will be.'

'And what of you? Shall you embrace my advice? Will you find out who you are by meeting with the Camerons and not hide from your fears?'

'I will follow your advice if you follow mine, my laird,' she answered with a smile. 'Agreed?'

'Agreed,' he replied.

The doubt that had tightened like a vice around his chest released him, and he took a full, heady breath before he seized her face in his hands and kissed her. He could feel the surprise on her lips, the shock of his actions in her lack of response at first. But then her lips softened against his own, her mouth yielding and answering his own desire with a matching ferocity. His hands slid back to the nape of her neck, weaving into the silky loose locks of her hair. Her arms slid around his shoulders, her fingertips skimming along his earlobes and neck, sending a crushing jolt of desire through him.

Had he ever felt such a response to a kiss?

Had she?

She shivered against him, and he stepped closer, pressing his body full along her own. Her solid, muscular frame nestled flush with his felt unholy yet necessary, a duality of feelings he was becoming accustomed to when it came to her. His lips claimed her own again and again as the smell of violets and wildflowers and the wind filled his nostrils. All too soon, she pulled away, resting her nose against the tip of his own.

'Well, my laird, I daresay that was a makeup kiss worth waiting for.'

'Aye. I would agree. Perhaps we should disagree more often.' He chuckled.

'Nay,' she answered. 'I find that I have missed you.'

'And I you.'

Chapter Twenty-One

As the carriage pulled out of the cobbled drive of Glen-haven, Catriona clutched her reticule to her stomach. She remained as uneasy as she had been when she'd rode in it for the first time weeks ago with nothing other than the clothes on her back, rescued by the strange laird who had purchased her. Ewan sat silently across from her, his gaze as unsettled as she felt. While they both wanted this visit to the Camerons, so she could truly know if they were her long-lost family or not, she couldn't shake her intuition. Something had changed between them, and she couldn't figure out what it was.

Ewan had been attentive and kind as they spent time together each day riding, and talking by the loch with Rufus. He also provided finger-numbing lessons with the clarsach, which she had yet to improve on. But something had been missing from his eyes since they had set the date for her to travel to the Camerons'. Doubt lingered there, and she had no idea why. They still planned to marry, and they'd had no more squabbles between them, so what had changed?

'Is something wrong, my laird?'

'Nay. Why?'

'You have changed since we set the date for our trip to Loch's End to see the Camerons. I thought you wanted me to do this. That you believed it was important to us both. Is it not?' she asked, twisting the ties of her reticule around her finger.

'It is. I am simply distracted by clan matters,' he answered, shifting on his seat.

She furrowed her brows. 'You can tell me anything. Just as we spoke of at the loch. I will always keep your secrets and share your burdens. We will be married soon, Ewan.' She reached across the seat and took his hand in hers.

He moved forward, his leg sliding between her own, holding her hands tightly. 'I have had this persistent fear that I will lose you once you set foot inside Loch's End. That you are a Cameron, and that you will see all they have to offer you as a family and realise that we... that I cannot provide you all you deserve. That you will choose another. Or that you will choose the life of independence and freedom you crave.'

She gripped his face between her hands. 'Have I said or done anything to make you believe such?'

'Nay,' he answered.

'Then tell me why you fear this.' She stroked his cheek with her fingers, and he pulled the palm of her hand to his mouth, kissing it, sending a thrill of heat and tingles along her entire body.

'Please, Ewan. Tell me the truth. I will understand.'

'Because of what happened with Emogene. She

showed me no signs of leaving either, and then one day she was just…gone. I fear it will be the same with you. I fear keeping you is impossible. That it is far too good to last.'

Aha. The pieces came together. It all made sense. Fear was driving him, not reason or his heart. Emogene had left her mark on him. She was why he had a rule about no romantic entanglements and not falling in love with his would-be wife. *She* was the one that made him balk at their connection and not trust it.

She smiled at Ewan. 'Thank you for telling me. It all makes perfect sense to me now, but you must know I am not her.'

He nodded. 'No, you aren't, and I am ever grateful for that and for you.'

'You are?'

'Aye. Shall I show you?' he asked, sliding even closer to her. His dimple emerged and flashed a warning she chose to ignore.

'I would like that,' she whispered, leaning forward, her hands resting on his thighs.

He picked up a tendril of her hair and let it slide through his fingers. 'I am grateful for your beautiful tresses, and your gorgeous cheeks.' He leaned in and pressed an achingly soft kiss to the apple of one of her cheeks and then the other. 'As well as your amber eyes and forehead.' He kissed her forehead and then made his way to her ears. 'And your ears.' When his lips skimmed the gentle part of her lobe, she gasped.

'Shall I stop?' he murmured in her ear.

'Nay,' she choked out, and she felt his smile against

her neck before he kissed it once and then twice before tracing the top of her exposed shoulder with his lips. She moaned and clutched at the nape of his neck. 'Kiss me,' she ordered.

He hoisted her onto his lap and kissed her. Not soft gentle kisses, but deep, thorough kisses that seared through her body one after another. His hands caressed her bodice, his fingertips skimming over the tops of her breasts just often enough to make her crave more and shift closer and closer to the core heat of his body.

She'd never felt this kind of desire to be with a man, and it raged in her like a wildfire. Nor did Ewan seem able to control his need. His hand slid along her bare ankle up her knee and then along her thigh. She thought she might squeal with pleasure at the fiery trail his touch created, and she tugged his tunic out of his trews, running her palm along his bare back. He groaned and shifted her closer until she thought she might shatter in his arms.

Bloody hell. What was he doing?

What had begun as a tease and way to rekindle their attraction to one another after days of discomfort between them had transformed quickly into something Ewan could scarcely control. His passion and craving for her burned hotter and brighter than any he'd ever known. She lifted her leg, allowing him better access as he clutched her thigh and kissed her, and the movement shook him into awareness.

He wanted her more than he'd ever wanted a woman in his whole life and…his body tightened…*and he loved her.*

The realisation landed on him like an ice bath, and he pulled back.

'I am sorry,' he sputtered, gripping her by the waist and moving her back to her bench seat. His breath was ragged, and the air between them in the carriage was charged with desire. Her face was flushed with colour, and she could not have been more enchanting. He had half a mind to ignore the logic commanding him to control himself and give in to the need coursing madly through his veins.

'Is something wrong?' she asked, her eyes searching his own for answers. Answers he could not give her without revealing the full truth of his feelings for her, which he wasn't ready to confess. He'd revealed enough to her today, had he not? Too much for his liking. He clamped down his jaw, tucked in his tunic, and looked away. Everything was wrong despite everything being so right. How could he explain such insanity to her?

He didn't even try, and thank the gods he didn't have to. The large Cameron estate, Loch's End, rose in an impressive and towering display as they climbed the hillside on the well-maintained road, reminding him of why they were travelling in this blasted carriage anyway: to see if Catriona was a Cameron. He swallowed his fear. And if she was, would she still choose what he offered her as his future wife? Or would she choose the independence and freedom she had long sought and desired since the first day he met her?

There was no denying the weight of privilege and opportunity she would have if it turned out that she was the Lost Girl of decades ago.

He faced her and forced a tight smile. 'We are here. Ready yourself,' he suggested, pointing to her dishevelled hair and now-twisted bodice of her gown. 'I should not have allowed myself to take advantage. My apologies,' he rushed out, avoiding her gaze entirely as he brushed off imaginary dirt from his finest jacket.

An odd quiet consumed the carriage. He could hear her muttering something under her breath, no doubt curses at him, as she adjusted her gown and pinned loose locks of her hair back into their plait. When had he become such a cad and prude all at the same time? Today, evidently. He sighed and berated himself once more. This was not how he had hoped their journey together to the Camerons' would go this morn. He'd hoped to chat with her to help her relax and deliver her with a clarity of heart and mind that would allow her to enjoy her brief stay with them, but also reassure her of his steadfast care and support for her and their future together. Instead, he had bungled everything.

He'd touched his future wife improperly, halted his advance without warning, and was about to deliver her to one of the most cunning and powerful clans in the Highlands unprepared. He rubbed the back of his neck. What should he do now?

'Would you like me to stay after all?' he fumbled out. 'I know we both thought it best for you to be there without me so you could focus your energies on seeing if they or Loch's End triggered any memories, but I'm sure I can stay if that would make you more comfortable.'

'Nay. I will be fine on my own. I will send word to you day after tomorrow,' she said. Her tone was sharp, a clear sign that his misstep was as bad as he suspected. 'You have made your fears clear, and I am seeing how they are ruling over you. I can do without such distraction during my visit.'

'Catriona,' he began. 'I am sorry, I—'

'We will speak of it later,' she interrupted as she smoothed her gown.

'I will plan to send on the carriage in two days' time to retrieve you and bring you back to Glenhaven. I am sure Rufus will be despondent about your absence by then,' he said, attempting to add some levity to the situation.

She was having no part of it. Her gaze flicked up and met his. As the carriage came to a rolling stop, she said, 'I will let you know *if* and when I am ready to be retrieved, my laird.'

He stilled. '*If* you wish to be retrieved?'

'Aye. You make *me* uncertain. I am battling a ghost from your past. I am not Emogene. Love and happiness are not to be feared. Nor am I. If my affection and care for you are too much, then you must decide that. I cannot, my laird.'

Before he could say a word, Aaron opened the carriage door.

'My laird,' Catriona stated with a nod. 'I will send word. Thank you for accompanying me. There is no need for you to escort me inside. I know you have much to attend to.' She accepted Aaron's hand to assist her to the cobbled drive and headed to the front door. Aaron followed behind her carrying her traveling bag for her brief stay at Loch's End. Ewan alighted from the carriage, trying to decide whether to follow her or call out for her return. Surely they couldn't leave things between them like this?

She continued, the distance growing between them, until she'd disappeared behind a bevy of soldiers who guarded the main entrance to the castle. His heart dropped to his stomach as he lost sight of her and realised she'd not glanced back to see if he was behind her as she'd walked on, not even once.

'Shall we return to Glenhaven, my laird, or shall I bring the carriage to the end of the drive and wait?' Aaron asked as he approached, having already deposited Catriona's bag to the footman. Uncertainty registered in his words.

Ewan came back to the moment and steeled his features. 'Aye,' he answered. 'We will return home. Evidently I am not needed here.'

He climbed back in the carriage, settled back into the squabs, closed his eyes, and cursed.

Chapter Twenty-Two

Catriona squashed the anger bubbling in her chest as she heard the Stewart carriage rolling down the lane behind her setting out to return to Glenhaven with Ewan in it.

Blasted man.

One minute he was bringing her to the brink of pleasure, and the next he had set a distance between them as large as the Moray Firth.

Men.

She shook off her frustration as she approached one of the Cameron soldiers at the double doors. She blinked as she brought herself back to the present moment and realised where she was and what she was about to do. She might be meeting her family. A family lost to her. And this sprawling castle was their home.

Could this be *her* home? If Glenhaven had impressed, Loch's End overwhelmed. It appeared to be at least twice the size and reflected all the hallmarks of wealth and power, as well as a focus on defence. Large towers buttressed corners of the huge stone structure with numerous square and Gothic windows, a few of which looked to be battlement-ready. The glass reflected the sunlight beaming down on the dark grey stone fortress. The Cameron coat of arms stood carved proudly above the door, a sheaf of five arrows tied with a band. Before she could take in more, the huge wooden double doors reinforced with iron strips groaned open.

Susanna Cameron stood flanked by the two soldiers that had opened the doors at her side and smiled. She looked every bit the sister of the laird in her forest-green gown, dark hair woven with a golden ribbon through her exquisite plait, and unyielding confidence. 'Come in, Mrs Gordon,' she said. 'It is about time you came home to us.'

The woman's faith in Catriona's lineage far outweighed her own. She nodded a greeting, walked up the large stone steps, and set foot into Loch's End. As the doors sealed closed behind her, Catriona paused, clutching her reticule as if it was life itself. What was she doing here? This spectacular place could not possibly be her home, could it? The entrance had smooth stone floors of a light grey, and two stained glass windows stretched above her. Colourful light streamed in on the stone. Below the windows was a vast staircase leading to the upper levels, and to the left and right of her were large open corridors covered in lush rugs, armoury, and the occasional flash of colour. Loch's End appeared to be as strong and formidable as the Camerons themselves.

'My brothers are awaiting us,' Susanna stated. 'Follow me.'

She had a strange way of phrasing orders as if they were invitations, and Catriona fell into step behind the woman's quick, purposeful stride. Catriona attempted to take in her surroundings but was distracted by her nerves and the pace at which they walked. Before she knew it, they waited outside another large wooden door. Susanna lifted the huge iron knocker and let it fall not once, but twice.

'Enter,' a man stated.

Catriona's heart pounded in her chest.

Susanna pushed the door open, and two men looked up at them. One of them paled as if he'd seen a ghost while the other gasped.

'Lord above,' the younger man murmured as he studied Catriona. He ran a palm down his face as he approached. Standing before her, his eyes welled, and he croaked out, 'Violet, it is you.'

'I… I am Catriona,' she stated as she looked upon him, self-conscious under his assessing gaze and the emotion he was struggling to control.

"I am Rolf," he replied. He was a handsome young man, a few years her junior, with soft blue eyes like his sister's and wild, wavy black hair.

'I…' he started, then cleared his throat. 'I am sure it is you.' He dug something out of his trouser pocket and held his hand closed before her. 'May I?' he asked, gesturing to her hands.

She nodded, extending a shaky hand to him.

'I have waited a long time to return this to you.' He cupped his hand with hers and placed a small piece of blue-green sea glass in it. Her heart pounded in her chest at the sight of it: the very piece she remembered finding that day at the beach and giving to her brother. Could this man have been her brother then? Could he be her brother now?

'It was many years ago when you pressed this wee bit of sea glass in my hand, sister. It was the last day I ever saw you. I have missed you, Vi,' he whispered, his voice husky and low, as he closed her hand over the sea glass and held it in his own.

Vi.

Suddenly, a flash of memory consumed her…

'Do not cry, brother,' she said.

'There are other shells. That one was just taken back by the ocean. What of this sea glass?' she asked, showing it to him.

Her brother wiped his eyes and sniffed before taking the small piece of glass worn smooth by the ocean from her hand.

'It is yours,' she said. *'My gift to my favourite brother,'* she whispered, and ruffled his hair.

He laughed and leaned into her side and hugged her. 'You are my favourite, too,' he said.

A tear spilled down her cheek. 'I remember now. You were sad at having lost a shell to the tide. And I found this and gave it to you.'

'You remember?' he asked.

She shook her head. 'I didn't until this very moment upon seeing it, seeing you…' Her throat clogged. 'Brother.'

She threw her arms around his neck, and he held her tight. 'Sister,' he whispered. 'I always knew we would find you. I never gave up. Never,' he said, holding her close.

'I knew it was you,' Susanna said, smiling at them. 'You see, Royce? We are reunited as a family at last. I am only sorry Mother and Father could not have been here to see it.' She wiped a tear from her cheek. 'Rolf, let me hug our sister. You have had her long enough,' she teased and batted him on the arm.

'Rolf,' Catriona whispered, pulling out of their embrace to look at her brother, wiping a tear from her cheek. It was hard to reconcile the small boy she knew with this young man, but it was him.

'Aye. That is me. Your baby brother,' he offered. 'And this is Royce, our oldest brother and now laird of the clan.'

Catriona's gaze met Royce's. His face gave away no emotion, his hard, unflinching features a sign that he was not as moved by her return or his siblings' joy at seeing her.

She nodded to him. 'Brother,' she said.

'Violet,' he replied with his arms crossed against his chest, his cool brown eyes assessing her.

'Please call me Catriona. It was the name Nettie gave me. She found me unconscious along the shore of Lismore and raised me. I could not remember my name or age, so she gifted me the name of Catriona and decided upon my age, which based on what you have said appeared to be correct.' She worried her hands.

'Royce, what is plaguing you? Our sister has returned. Greet her,' Rolf chided.

Royce moved to her and hugged her, his embrace rigid and void of any feeling, much like she was hugging a large boulder. Catriona stepped back quickly, feeling awkward and unsure after such a warm greeting from her other siblings.

Had something happened between them?

'Thank you for allowing me to visit, my laird,' she offered, attempting to appeal to his position. It seemed the safest way through.

'Aye. We had to know if you were our sister.' He pointed to her wrist. 'And now we are sure of it.'

She looked at her wrist and met his gaze, puzzled by his words. 'That is a scar from attempting to help cook slice up the fruit for a dessert.' He almost smiled.

She examined it. 'Oh, I did not know.'

'I will take my leave. I have clan matters to attend to. I will see you at dinner.' And with that Royce was gone.

Catriona bit her lip. Was it something she said or didn't say?

'Pay no mind to Royce,' Rolf said, casting a glance towards the door. 'He has been in a foul mood for the last decade.'

'Aye,' Susanna offered. 'It isn't you. Come, let us show you Loch's End, and then we can sit down and talk. We've much to catch up on.'

She slipped Catriona's arm through her own and guided her out with Rolf by her side.

While she'd started the day as an orphan, she would end the day with a family, and the realisation of it stung her eyes.

Catriona and her siblings sat outside in the garden, watching the sun set over the loch. Even Royce had joined them, which had pleased her more than she wished to admit.

'So, how did you even come to know Laird Stewart?' Rolf asked. Catriona shifted in her chair. She knew the question would come up eventually as she'd already spent a great deal of time recounting Nettie's rescue of her along the shore, her brief time at the Arrans, and her years as a servant for the Chisholms. She'd counted her blessings that this hadn't been the first topic of conversation at dinner. Attempting to heed some of her own advice, she said the truth of it.

Taking a steadying breath, she met Rolf's gaze and answered.

'My husband, Thomas, was selling me off in the Grassmarket. Laird Stewart offered to buy me.'

They stared at her in abject horror before Royce spoke first. 'Stewart *bought* you? You are a woman, not a mare.'

The anger in his voice cut through the night air, and her heart pounded in her chest. She stuttered out a reply. 'He…he did it to save me. Another man, whom he knew to be cruel, was about to buy me instead, so he stepped in to rescue me. That is all.'

'Who was this other man?' he asked.

'Dallan MacGregor.'

Royce stood, put his hands on his hips, and turned away from them. One curse and then another carried across the breeze, and no one spoke.

'And Laird Stewart's treatment of you since then?' he asked, finally facing them again. Was that anguish or rage she saw in his eyes?

'He has been a kind and generous host. His actions freed me from my husband, Thomas, which I am grateful for.'

'And you plan to marry him?' Susanna asked. 'Are you even free to do so?'

'Aye. Laird Stewart's solicitor was checking into the matter for us, as we did not know if the agreement was even legal. He discovered that even though Laird Stewart purchased me, I was still legally married to Thomas.'

'So, if you cannot marry after all, why was there a celebration of your engagement just last week?' Royce asked.

Catriona shifted again in her seat. 'In searching for my husband, the solicitor found he had been killed by the husband of a woman he was…seeing. I am now a widow and free to remarry.'

He ran a hand through his hair. 'I've never heard of anything so crass.'

'It seems horrible, I know, but I am happy to be free of Thomas. He was…he was not a kind man, even though he did provide me food and shelter. I did not wish him such a horrible death, but I am grateful to no longer be his wife.' She looked down at her hands, tracing the scars along her knuckles.

'Are those from him?' Rolf asked gently, following the direction of her gaze.

She looked to him. 'Only some of them.'

'I can take no more of this,' Royce said, rising abruptly from his seat along the stone wall where they sat. 'We will finish our discussion tomorrow. Good night.' He nodded to them and left, disappearing into the darkening sky.

Blast.

Catriona pressed her lips together in a thin line and worried the edge of her shawl. She'd upset the man again. It was one misstep after another with him. What was she doing wrong?

'He will come around,' Rolf said. 'We are happy you are here and hope you will stay as long as you like.'

'I don't know if Royce would agree to that,' Catriona answered with a slight chuckle. 'He seems…quite unsettled by my presence, and he is the laird, after all.'

'Who cares what he wants?' Susanna answered, standing up and stretching. 'The two of us outnumber him. Don't we, Rolf?' She laughed, reached out, and squeezed Catriona's hand. 'Why don't I show you your chambers, and you can get settled in. You must be exhausted. I know I am.'

'Aye. That would be lovely,' Catriona answered. She stood and stifled a yawn. 'Thank you both for being so welcoming. It is a great deal to take in all at once. I try not to think of all I have lost without you but choose to focus on what awaits us in the future instead.'

'I am just glad you have been returned to us,' Rolf added. 'That day you disappeared, we searched and searched for you. Word was sent to all the clans, and all searched for you as well. We returned there every month, then every year, still hoping to find you, even though we knew you had been taken by the sea. And here you are, returned to us in the same fashion as if you were dropped by the heavens.' He stared out at the horizon.

She followed his gaze and stared out into the loch, its waters lapping softly below. 'I see why this place is called Loch's End. You feel like you are at the edge of the universe. You can see to forever from up here.' And she could. The loch joined the sea, and nothing seemed beyond it but horizon and sky. It made the world seem full of possibilities she'd never even imagined for herself.

'Well, this is your new beginning here, Vi—' Susanna paused '—I mean, Catriona. Think of this as you starting a new life with your old family. Not many people get second chances. I know we will not waste our second chance with you, will we, Rolf?'

'Nay. We won't,' he answered. 'We've missed out on so much of your life. Tomorrow, we will show you the rest of the grounds, so you can see what your life here could be as sister of the laird. As a Cameron.'

She fell in step with them as they walked along, enjoying the fine sights and smells of the garden in the eve. Catriona's stomach flipped at the idea of having more choices. She could scarcely manage the new ones that had been thrust upon her since leaving the Grassmarket and going to Glenhaven.

Glenhaven. Ewan.

It would be the first night she was not under his roof in over three weeks. It was an odd and heady sensation. She missed him. She knew that. But an inkling of an idea was forming as she stared out at the horizon.

Could she finally be free and independent, as she'd

always wanted, as a Cameron? Could she choose to be under no one's control but her own?

Perhaps that would be best for a man like Ewan, who did not want to risk love, and for a woman like her, who finally wanted to see what it was all about.

Chapter Twenty-Three

Ewan grumbled at his writing desk and tossed yet another spoiled piece of parchment in the bin. At this rate, he would never finish balancing the ledgers and sending out enquiries about updating the salon for Catriona as a surprise wedding gift. He paused. He might not even need to. His fiancée seemed to have disappeared by all accounts. Just as he had feared.

Just like Emogene.

He loosened his cravat. Or perhaps his horrid behaviour had driven her away. He cursed at the memory of almost bedding his wife-to-be in a bloody carriage on their way to the Camerons'. He'd then been an arse and pushed her away with no explanation for his behaviour. All because he feared loving her. *Fool.* He loved her already, and nothing would change that. All the lies he could tell himself would not make the truth different or the utter fear such a truth created in him less real.

His pulse increased. And now, he didn't know what to do for he'd ruined it all. He glanced out of the window. Lightning flashed, and then thunder boomed off in the distance. His temper was as foul as the dark looming clouds that hung over the valley and the loch. Catriona had been gone for four days without a single word. He'd sent one polite enquiry about when to retrieve her after two days had passed, but his letter had gone unanswered, and his pride refused to allow him to send another. He was a laird, after all. The only communication he had received at all from Loch's End was a letter from Royce stating that she was indeed their sister.

Mrs Catriona Gordon was the long-lost Violet Cameron.

'Is this your plan?' Brenna asked, leaning against the door frame of his study, yanking Ewan from his thoughts.

'Plan for what?' he asked, his irritation blooming back up at his sister's meddling.

'To get Catriona back, of course. What else would I possibly be referring to?'

'Is she lost?' he said, sarcasm dripping off his words.

Brenna came into the room, closing the door loudly behind her. 'You and I both know that if you do nothing, she will never return from Loch's End. She will stay with the Camerons indefinitely. What is wrong with you? I know you love her. Why are you sitting here doing nothing?' Her voice was high and infused with emotion.

He matched her fervour, stood at his desk, and leaned forward. 'Of course I care for her. I love her, which is the whole problem,' he answered, exasperated by the truth and by his weakness. Why could he tell his sister, but not the woman he loved, how much he cared for her?

'So, you admit you *love* her?' she said softly.

'Aye. So much so that I feel absolutely ill at the thought of it.' He slumped back into his chair, tugged the cravat from his neck, and tossed it on the desk amidst the disarray already there.

Not much mattered any more without Catriona here.

Brenna approached him and gifted him a sympathetic smile. 'Then do something about it.'

'Like what?' He shrugged. 'I sent word to her, but my letter went unanswered.'

'Do you know if she even received it?' She leaned against the desk beside him, staring out at the dark rolling clouds. 'You know the Camerons. Royce may be holding her correspondence until they have a better handle on the situation. They may be as desperate to keep her there as we are to have her returned to us, especially after they had lost her for so long.'

'Aye. They might be.'

'Go to her. Fetch your bride-to-be. *Show* her how much you care for her.' She nudged him and smiled.

'And if she will not see me?'

'Then you will have your answer and at least be out of this horrid misery. Although I might suggest a bath first,' she added, sniffing him.

He nudged her back. 'You are such a burden, sister, but I adore you. Even if you plague me beyond measure.'

'What else are sisters for? Besides, be grateful Moira was not here. She would have harangued you even more, and you know it. You would have been begging for mercy.'

He nodded. 'You are right.'

There was a knock at the door. 'Come in,' Ewan called.

'Just arrived for you, my laird.' Mrs Stevens smiled holding a letter. 'From Mrs Gordon, I believe.'

'Ah, perhaps you may not need to pay a visit after all, brother.' Brenna beamed at Mrs Stevens and sent Ewan a wink.

Ewan's heart soared as he rose to accept the letter. 'Thank you, Mrs Stevens.'

She nodded, stepped out, and left them.

The letter had some weight to it, and he furrowed his brow. 'Heavy,' he said as he turned it over in his hand and broke the seal. He frowned when he saw the Cameron crest had been pressed into the wax. A sign that Royce had been involved in the sending of her correspondence. That didn't bode well, did it?

Royce and Rolf had still not forgiven him for what had happened to one of their beloved stallions along their small section of shared border wall that the Stewarts were tasked with maintaining. The horse had escaped through a portion of collapsed stone and not returned. Most likely seized by whomever had been lucky enough to find him. Rolf had dislocated his shoulder in an attempt to chase down the beast. He fell down a ravine trying to prevent its escape. Despite feeling that the Camerons had been at fault by letting it free from their stables, Ewan had repaid them in kind with a fine gelding last spring.

He took a tentative breath and released it. He unfolded the letter, and upon seeing a guinea, he faltered.

He turned over the worn coin in his fingers before setting it aside on his desk. He swallowed hard and read on:

To my dearest Laird Stewart,
I cannot thank you enough for what you have done to free me from my previous situation. You, and you alone, rescued me from my husband in that horrid market square that morning in Edinburgh, and you brought me back to the Highlands knowing nothing about who I was or my past. If I had never returned here, I would not have ever found the family lost to me, the Camerons, and been reunited with my siblings. I am indebted to you for your kindness and for bringing me back to my family and to a life I never would have known otherwise.

Enclosed is a guinea to repay you for the debt I owe you for purchasing my freedom from my husband that day. I hope this will cancel my financial debt to you as it is now repaid in full. I also wish to end our attachment to one another as future husband and wife as I cannot promise to live the rest of my days married to a man as glorious as you knowing I am not allowed to love you.

I have lived far too much of my life without love. Now that I know how precious and beautiful it is, I refuse to deny myself another day of it.

I respect that you do not feel the same, and I wish you every happiness in your quest to find a woman who can match your desire for a marriage of convenience without love. This would have been enough for the old me...for Mrs Ca-triona Gordon...but it is not enough for me now.

It is not enough for the new me.

With gratitude and love in my heart for you always,

Catriona Violet Cameron

Also, please tell Brenna and Betsy that I will be in touch, and give Rufus, Starlight, and Wee Bit a pet. I will miss them too.

If he'd thought it possible for his heart to stop and for him to still be alive, he would have said that was what happened to him. For he could not breathe or feel anything other than anguish over her words. She had rejected him. She had let him go. Not for more power or wealth, but because he had refused to allow her to love him and him to love her. The very thing he feared would happen, he had created in his own quest for control, and it could not be undone.

'Leave me,' he said.

'Brother? What has happened?' Brenna asked.

'If you care for me at all, sister, you will leave me be. Now. I need to be alone.' His words were hollow and flat, devoid of the raging emotion tightening his chest.

Lightning lit up the sky, and thunder shook the castle. He turned away from her searching gaze. Shortly after, he heard the door open and then close, as softly as a whisper.

He turned to his desk, overflowing with books, papers, and everything else in between. He placed his palms flat on the cool wood, forced a few breaths, and yelled in frustration before sending all the contents on top of his desk crashing to the floor. Panting, he took to the walls, ripping down maps and swords, revelling in the destruction and noise. By the time he was finished, his father's pristine and orderly study was in ruins, and Ewan felt like his surroundings finally matched the chaos within him.

Catriona paced under the covered walkway outside the castle walls, tugging her shawl closer as the winds increased. A storm raged over the loch just as doubt raged within her heart. She'd sent the letter as Royce had encouraged her to do to end this farce of an engagement with Ewan. She knew it was the only way for her to clearly assess her options for the future and decide what she wanted for herself now that she was a Cameron. She could stay at Loch's End as long as she wanted until she remarried, and neither of her brothers seemed in any rush to marry her off. They were both plagued by what had happened to her, so much so that they struggled to say the words out loud.

When she'd asked Royce for the guinea to include in the letter as repayment for what Ewan had spent to safely rescue her from her husband and Dallan Mac-Gregor, he'd blanched at first. He'd paled and left her but returned a few minutes later. He'd lifted her hand gently and pressed a guinea into it without a word, but the sorrow in his eyes was unmistakable. She hoped one day she could speak with him about it, but it didn't appear that it would be anytime soon. Her eldest brother was the most guarded man she'd ever met and kept his emotions close.

Unlike Rolf. She smiled at the thought of her younger brother. He was kind and gentle, and wasn't afraid to show his emotion. If anything, he might be too open to the world, and Catriona felt fiercely protective of him despite only knowing him as an adult for a handful of days. Susanna proved to be a much softer soul as well, although in front of others outside of their family, she was quite formidable, ruling with clarity of purpose and finality. At the moment, all Catriona had was doubt about her decision regarding Ewan. Had she done the right thing in sending that letter to him?

She didn't know.

'What are you doing out here?' Susanna asked. 'A storm is coming. Join me inside.'

'I cannot rest after sending that letter to Ewan. I do not know if I did the right thing.'

Susanna narrowed her gaze. 'What letter?'

'I sent a letter to Ewan to repay him for my freedom and Royce encouraged me to also sever our engagement, so I did.'

Susanna's eyes widened. She clutched Catriona by the arm and hustled her inside. 'Not a word until we reach my chamber,' she hissed, almost dragging Catriona down one hallway and then the next. Their L-shaped castle was deceptively larger on the inside than it even appeared on the outside. Once inside the chamber, its lavender-coloured walls a calming haven, Catriona collapsed into one of her sister's oversized chairs with its floral pattern.

'What are you talking about? What letter?' Susanna

asked, removing her slippers and settling into the chair opposite Catriona. She leaned back and drew down the bell pull behind her to call for a servant. 'Would you like anything besides tea?'

'Nay,' she answered. 'I've not much of an appetite.'

'You didn't at dinner either. Tell me why. What has our dear older brother done now?' The sharpness in her tone sent alarm through Catriona. This was the first time she'd heard Susanna speak ill of their brother. She'd teased him about his difficult and rather cool personality, but there hadn't been any malice laced in her words...until now.

'We were talking about my engagement to Ewan,' Catriona said, running the fringe of her shawl through her fingertips. 'He encouraged me to rethink my promise to Laird Stewart, since my situation had changed. He was looking out for me. He didn't wish for me to make a hasty decision, especially now that I know I am a Cameron and have more options for my future.'

'More options?' she scoffed, a note of bitterness in her words. 'What he means is more options for him as laird. I wish you had spoken to me first, sister, but it is too late now.'

Catriona stilled. 'What do you mean, more options for him as a laird?'

She chuckled. 'I know you are acquainted with the ways of the world, sister. You know that women have little say in their future. You were sold, for heaven's sake.'

Catriona's body flushed with heat, and she looked away.

Susanna leaned forward. 'I do not mean to embarrass you. That is not my intent. I just want you to understand that women have as little power in families of wealth and privilege as they do in homes of poverty. We are pawns to be used for advantage. Nothing more.' She smiled sympathetically. 'The only card you held with my brother was your engagement to Laird Stewart as you had decided upon it yourself, and you have just given that up. Which I believe is exactly what Royce wanted.'

Catriona fought to keep her emotions under control as she searched the castle for her eldest brother, Royce. Susanna had begged her to wait and speak with him in the morn when she was in a better temper, but Catriona had ignored such advice. A servant had encouraged her to seek him out in the armoury, which seemed an odd place to be so late at night. As she rounded the corner and stepped into the room, she saw the man had been right. Royce sat on one of the rock benches as he sharpened a dirk with a whetstone in smooth, rhythmic strokes. The sight of it calmed some of her anger because it piqued her curiosity.

'Couldn't you have a soldier or servant do that for you?' she asked.

Royce ceased his movements, glanced at her, and then continued the steady, recurrent strokes of the stone against the metal. 'I prefer to not trust anyone else to sharpen my blades.'

The sound was oddly soothing, and Catriona felt her temper soften more. She sat next to him and watched for a moment before she asked what had been so pressing moments ago. 'Should I be worried that you will marry me off for the most advantageous match now that I have broken my promise with Laird Stewart?'

He sighed and set aside the stone, dirk, and cloth beside him. 'Has Susanna been speaking with you?' His dark brown eyes searched hers.

Catriona nodded an answer.

'She is hurt by her past. There was a lad she wished to marry, but Father forbade it. Since then, she has resisted every effort to find her a husband. No doubt, she fears the same for you.'

'You did not answer my question.'

He smiled. 'You always were quick. You wish to hear the truth?'

'I would prefer it,' she replied.

He turned his body to face her. 'I *do* wish to find you the best match for your future as well as the future of the clan. That is my duty as your brother and laird, and I can assure you that a union with Laird Ewan Stewart is not such a match. His clan will fall soon. Whether by the British, another clan, or infighting, I do not know, but they will not last. Not without help.' His words were even and unfettered by anything other than logic and reason. While his words shook her to the bone, he was unmoved, as if they were speaking of what new flowers to plant in the back garden.

She shivered. The man had ice running through his veins.

'And if I decide I was wrong, and that I should not have broken off my engagement to him?'

He turned forward, picked up his dirk and whetstone

and began to sharpen the blade once more. After five or six strokes, he paused and looked at her. 'Then you will be digging your own grave, sister. Mark my words. Love is unimportant in such matters. You will see.'

She rose from her seat and backed out of the room, feeling queasy. Digging her own grave? Those weren't exactly the words of support and approval she had been searching for. What did she do now? And who did she believe?

Maybe she'd been better off with few choices. Having this many made her feel addled and confused.

Chapter Twenty-Four

'You would think you were going to a funeral rather than the greatest ball of the summer season,' Susanna teased as she adorned each of Catriona's ears with the most gorgeous emerald drop earrings Catriona had ever seen. They caught the candlelight from her dressing table and glimmered.

She stilled her sister's hands. 'I cannot wear these, Susanna. They are too beautiful. What if I lose one?'

'They were Mother's, and I insist. She would want you to have them. They match your gown to perfection, and the jewellery appears made for you. Look how it brings out the green and gold flecks in your eyes and the roses in your cheeks.' She kissed her cheek.

'I wish I could remember her and Father. I look upon their portrait, but they seem like someone else's parents. Not mine.' She glanced at the small portrait of her parents that Rolf had moved into her room. He wanted her to see if it might trigger a memory of them.

It hadn't. Not yet, anyway.

Susanna sat down next to Catriona on the small bench

seat before the gilded mirror above her dressing table. 'Remembering them does not matter as much as knowing that they loved you beyond measure. Mother spoke of you as long as Father would allow it.'

Catriona balked. 'He did not allow her to speak of me?'

'Father was quite like Royce. Closed up, distant when it related to matters of the heart. I believe losing you affected him so much that about two years after you disappeared, he forbade us to speak of you in front of him entirely.' She sighed. 'It became something special between us and Mother. We would talk of what we remembered of you and what we imagined you might be doing. We never allowed ourselves to believe you were dead, but merely elsewhere living your life.'

A tear ran down Catriona's cheek. 'You spoke of me?'

'Often. Daily at first and then less over time. Sometimes it was too painful, but other times we would laugh over the creative stories we would craft for your new life.'

'You did?' Catriona wiped her cheek. 'What were some of them?'

Susanna chuckled. 'My favourite was one Rolf came up with. He believed you had developed powers as a witch and healer. A good witch, of course, and that you were able to travel through time to watch over us when you wished. He missed you the most. He was utterly lost without you for some time. To see you two together now—' she pressed a hand to her chest '—fills my heart more than I thought possible.' Her eyes welled with tears.

Catriona clutched one of her sister's hands in her own. 'I am sorry for all the time we have lost, but I am grateful to have found you. To have the time with you now. It is a gift I never thought possible. To have a family again.'

'And you shall always have us, no matter what Royce may have said to you.'

Catriona shrugged. 'He did not say I had to choose between Ewan or being a Cameron.'

'He did not encourage you to marry the man either.'

'Nay.' She chuckled. 'He did not. He warned me of what he believed to be the demise of the Stewarts and suggested that I may be tethering myself to a man and a people that will be destroyed in a few years' time. But I cannot fathom it. Glenhaven is large and thriving. It is not as impressive as Loch's End, but I cannot imagine it disappearing or being overcome.'

'I know it seems impossible, but you have met Brenna's fiancé, Garrick MacLean, have you not?'

'Aye,' said Catriona.

'Well, no one may have told you, but that is exactly what happened to him and his people. Over the course of a year and a half, he lost his family, his ancestral home of Westmoreland, and his clan.'

'Why?' she asked, sitting straighter. Laird MacLean appeared a good and competent man. What could have changed that?

'The British. When he was away, his family refused to pay the taxes due. The soldiers made an example of the MacLeans to keep the other clans in line.'

Catriona swallowed hard. She needed no further explanation of what all that might entail. Although she had lived in the south of Scotland for most of her life, she had heard the stories of destruction in the Highlands and had an idea of what had befallen his family and his people.

'And Royce believes that may happen to Ewan and the Stewarts?'

'Perhaps. But Royce always prepares for the worst. It is one of the things that makes him a great laird, believe it or not.' Susanna smiled.

'I hope he is wrong,' said Catriona.

'Aye,' she agreed. 'So do I. But you do not need to make your decision about your happiness based on one man's supposed prediction. It is also not too late for you to repair things with Laird Stewart if you wish it. He will be here tonight. And when he sees you, he will lose all reason.'

Catriona bit her lip. She had tried to forget that he would be here this eve, but there was no avoiding it. 'I do not know what I wish, sister, which is part of my dilemma. I love him, but he does not want love. He wants an arrangement without complications. He told me so the first night I was at Glenhaven, but I cannot go back to having less. I want to marry a man who loves me and will accept my love in return.'

'Have you told him this?'

'I did in the letter I sent him. Most of it, anyway.'

'Perhaps tell him tonight in person. Talk about it. Talk about all of it. Love is not so easy to find. Trust me on this. If I had another chance with the man I loved, I would seize it.'

'And if he decides we are not meant to be after all?'

'Then you will know you had tried. I wish I could say the same.' Susanna touched up her hair and added more colour to Catriona's lips. Sadness showed in Susanna's eyes. 'You will make him swoon. You will make them all swoon, my dear. The choice will be yours.'

Nerves fluttered in Catriona's stomach. 'So, what is this ball we are hosting, and who shall be here?'

'It is the Grand Highlander Ball. The finest celebration of the season. Held here of course, since we have the largest holdings. Royce invites all the clan lairds as well as elders with a few influential merchants and men in industry from Edinburgh. We celebrate the year before and prepare for the one to come.'

Catriona lifted her brow to her. 'Which means?'

Susanna smiled. 'Many deals and alliances are forged, marriage matches agreed upon, ghastly amounts of food and wine consumed, and much dancing had by all. You will love it.'

Catriona laughed. It didn't sound so bad now.

'And you don't have to ride endlessly in a carriage to get there. All you need do is walk downstairs. The music will begin any minute now.'

And as she spoke the words, the fiddles and lutes began to play. 'That is our cue. We are to greet guests as they arrive.'

Catriona froze. 'What?'

'I know,' she said sheepishly. 'I should have warned you before now, but I feared you would claim a megrim and not come down. Once word spreads that you have returned to us, no one else will ask how or why. No man would dare challenge Royce about the matter. They are not fools. They know he can crush any clan here if he wishes it. We have enough power on our own, but we also have more alliances and debts owed to us than all the other clans in the Highlands combined.'

'How is that possible?'

'We know how to utilise advantages when they come our way.' She winked at her with a wicked smile.

Catriona believed her on all counts and followed her older sister down to the corridor and staircase. They descended and stopped at the top of the landing, looking down into a small crowd of guests that had already arrived.

'Some of them you met at the gathering at Glenhaven, but for the others, keep your answers brief and to the point, and do not linger,' Susanna urged. 'Some of these lairds have hands with a mind of their own.'

'I'll remember that,' Catriona murmured. Her worries multiplied as every new person arrived. She had never seen so many elegant people in one place in all her life. Women wore gowns of the finest fabrics and extravagant jewels that caught the candlelight flickering along the wall and from the lit chandeliers above.

Catriona followed her sister down the stairs and headed to the large entryway. 'Go with Rolf,' Susanna whispered as she veered off to the left to stand next to Royce, whose gaze flicked up to her quickly and then away.

Catriona swallowed and stood next to Rolf. He grinned at her and whispered, 'You are stunning, sister. I am so happy to have you by my side this eve.' He squeezed her hand briefly and then let go.

His excitement and joy overshadowed her fears, and she smiled back at him. 'As am I you, brother.'

Greeting the guests wasn't as tortuous as she had expected, especially since only half of them came to greet her anyway. The guests fanned out into two streams upon arriving through the large double door entryway and greeted whichever pair of Cameron siblings happened to be on their side. Once Rolf introduced her as his long-lost sister, the guests were so overwhelmed with joy and celebration that none asked where she'd been found or where she'd been, which was a relief. Or at least, none dared ask in front of her. She didn't know exactly what she would have uttered in reply to such a question except for Edinburgh, which might not have been the full answer they would have expected.

Catriona heard Ewan before she saw him. He was greeting Royce and Susanna. His familiar smooth tone resonated through her ears and made her come alive. Even with his back to her, her body sang at the sight of him, and her fingers longed to touch him. She fought the urge to call to him, and when he moved out of the receiving line towards the main room, a sense of loss whirred through her. She reminded herself it was early as she stared after him. She would have the time she needed to speak with him and settle the discord between them.

'Perhaps you and Susanna would like to dance?' Rolf offered, following the direction of her gaze. 'Royce and I can handle the few guests that have not yet arrived.'

Catriona pressed a kiss to his cheek. 'Thank you, brother.'

Susanna mouthed a thank-you to Rolf as well, grabbed Catriona's hand, and whisked her away to the main hall, where the dancing was taking place. 'And now, we dance,' she said, shouting out a cheer of excitement. Catriona laughed and joined in the reel that was already happening. The revellers absorbed them into their dance with ease, and Catriona smiled. The night of her first ball, she'd found her family, and she wondered what she might find this eve on the night of her second.

Ewan watched Catriona across the room, and his heart filled with such pleasure. She danced and laughed in a bewitching green gown. Her hair was half pinned and half loose, and emerald earrings bobbed from her ears. He had never seen her so happy, so alive, and so free.

Freedom.

It was what she said she had wanted most that night when he'd intercepted her as she'd tried to flee Glenhaven. And now she had it in spades. She had a family, she had choices, and he couldn't begrudge her any of it. Despite the ache and longing in his chest and desire to have her as his own and as his wife, he was content to see her so blissfully happy after all she had been through before he'd met her that day in the Grassmarket.

'She appears happy,' Garrick said, sidling up next to Ewan.

'Aye. And as much as it crushes me to bits to no longer have her as my own, I am bewitched by her joy.'

'Then you, my laird, are in love.'

Ewan frowned. 'Are you here merely to plague me?'

'Maybe,' he said, elbowing Ewan in the side. 'And perhaps to encourage you to speak with her once more. To know for certain if things are truly ended between you or if this is just a misunderstanding.'

'I think she made it quite clear. I either risk loving her, or she is gone. There is no middle ground.'

'You already love her, and she you, if I am not mistaken. What is the risk?' Garrick asked.

'Utter ruin if she rejects me again. She cannot fully know what she wants. She has had nothing and been given the world. That is a drastic change for a short period of time. I should know. It was how I felt when I became laird. How I still feel about it.' He took a long drink from his tankard.

'But that is the beauty of it. You cannot control it, and the more you try, the more you will fail. You can take *my* word on that. Speak the truth to her and just be open to what happens.'

'You always make things sound so blasted simple, when they are nothing but.'

Garrick smirked. ''Tis a gift.'

'Or a curse,' he mused. He glanced back to where Catriona had been dancing and saw that she was gone.

'I will follow your advice, but now I must find her. I lost her in the reel.' He clapped his friend on the shoulder and headed off past the dancers.

Perhaps she sought refreshment or chose to take some air. The room was warming as the dancing continued and more and more guests arrived. Ewan stood in the centre of the room and scanned it for her with no luck. If he remembered correctly, the refreshments were in one direction down the hallway while the covered terrace where one could take in some air and look upon the loch was in the other. Which would Catriona choose?

Smiling, he set down his empty tankard on a side table and set out in the direction of the terrace, knowing how much she adored the night sky and the stars. If there was a place she might try to catch her breath in this throng of people, it was there. What did he have to lose?

He made his way through the first room without much difficulty, but then had quite the time carving a path through some elders recounting the days of their youth and sharing old battle stories and the wounds that accompanied them. Sidelined to hear the end of one such tale, he then carried on, eventually making his way to the terrace. He walked out onto the stone walkway with its cover and scanned the lit area, shadows flickering along the way.

His heart sank when he didn't find her there. Where could she be? He frowned. In Loch's End, the lass could be anywhere. The castle was expansive, and as family, she could travel anywhere amongst its massive maze of corridors and chambers. As a guest, there were only limited sections he could roam. Otherwise he would be at Royce's mercy. And he'd rather that not be added to the list of the man's grievances against him.

Ewan stepped back inside, and then stilled as he heard her voice. He smiled. Perhaps she had been taking some air and had returned only minutes before he had checked the area. No matter. He would talk with her now.

She was set off in a corner, speaking to one of the Stewart elders and his wife. They both smiled as she recounted of the joys of riding and how beautiful she found the daily outings she had taken in the valley. The way she spoke of it moved him. She talked of it with pride as if the land were hers. She spoke of it the way he felt about her in his heart.

As they wrapped up their conversation, Catriona turned in his direction and met his gaze. Although her smile faltered, her eyes brightened at the sight of him, and his heart thudded in his chest, his body feeling alive at being close to her again after so many days apart.

They walked towards each other, and he made a slight bow in greeting. 'Lady Cameron,' he said, acknowledging the change in her name after being claimed by the family as well as the respect she was due. 'You are enchanting this eve, as always.'

She blushed. 'You are too kind, my laird.' Her gaze held his. 'I have missed you.'

'And I you, Catriona,' he replied. 'May we speak?' he asked. 'About your letter…about us?' his voice dropped as he moved closer to her. He revelled in her familiar sweet smell.

'I would like that,' she said. He offered his arm to her, and she accepted. The feel of her hand sliding along his forearm soothed him. Maybe things could go back to where they were. Perhaps not all was lost between them.

'Stewart,' a man called from behind them as they made their way through the gathering. 'Is that you and your new bride?'

Bollocks.

Ewan bristled. He knew that voice. He let go of Catriona's arm and turned to face him.

'MacGregor,' Ewan replied. He glared at the man and walked towards him, placing himself between the bastard and Catriona.

Dallan sidestepped him and set his gaze on Catriona, letting his eyes roam slowly and shamelessly over her. She blushed under his gaze. 'I almost did not recognise you, my dear. But then, when I saw you two together and those bewitching eyes of yours, I remembered you from the market square.'

A few people around them quieted and took interest in their exchange, which was exactly what Dallan wanted. He'd never been good at losing to anyone. He did not care about the shame he would bring upon Catriona. He'd use this moment to embarrass the Camerons. Catriona would be an innocent victim among the carnage of what Ewan knew was coming.

'I am surprised to see you here,' Ewan said. 'Surely you were not invited after the outcome of last year's ball.' He stepped into the man's space and blocked Catriona from him.

'Invitations are no matter. I arrived with my own guest.' He gestured to an older matron of wealth off to the side. 'I don't need to bring rubbish that I find on the street with me.'

Rage flashed through Ewan, and he grabbed Dallan by the tunic. 'You will cease your slander, or I will throw you out myself.'

'What is going on here?' Royce asked. 'There will be no fighting at this celebration.'

'I cannot keep such a promise when you allow the likes of MacGregor in,' Ewan answered, letting go of the man.

'What do you mean?' Royce asked. He stopped short at the sight of Dallan. 'Aye. He must have come in late after we stopped greeting our guests. He is *not* welcome here.'

'I would think I'd be welcome considering what other trash you have allowed in and made a part of your family. Although I hardly recognise you without your harness, whore.'

'Whore?' Royce growled.

Ewan said nothing, but punched Dallan in the face, sending the man back into the sea of guests behind him and skidding to the floor.

The bastard regained his footing and smirked, wiping the blood from the corner of his mouth. 'She must be quite the minx in bed for you to risk peace between our people by fighting me so openly.'

'How dare you speak that way about my fiancée!'

'Your fiancée? You *bought* her, Stewart. I was there. She is your possession, I suppose, but nothing more. No matter how the Camerons dress her up and whatever new name they give her, you cannot change *what* she is, which is rubbish.'

Ewan charged into him, sending them both headlong into the crowd and sprawling onto the floor. He landed punch after punch to the man, unable to stop the fury coursing through his veins.

'Ewan!' Catriona screamed. 'Stop! You will kill him.'

Ewan only hoped he could as he took a blow to the

chin and one to the gut before continuing his assault on the bastard once more.

'Cease!' Royce ordered, dragging Ewan off Dallan with effort. 'If anyone kills him, it will be me. Rolf, have some men bring MacGregor to the armoury, where he will be dealt with. And have them take Stewart outside to cool off.'

Rolf waved over two Cameron soldiers and they dragged off Dallan, who was covered with blood but still arguing his point, through the crowd. The music in the other room still roared, the dancers oblivious to the chaos outside their revelry.

'Let me go,' Ewan argued, struggling against Royce, who had Ewan's arm pinned behind his back.

'Keep struggling and you will tear your shoulder in two,' Royce countered. 'Leave MacGregor to me. We will deal with him. She is our family now and not yours to defend.'

'She is my fiancée. I know what is best for her, and I will protect her.' Ewan stopped struggling, and Royce released him.

'Oh?' he said. 'I believe that attachment was ended, and your debt repaid.'

'Nay. She is my betrothed and under my care.'

'Nay,' Royce argued, gripping Ewan by his jacket, standing over him. 'She is my sister and under my care and protection. I will make her decisions for her, not you.'

Anger brewed once more in Ewan.

Before Ewan could throw a punch, Catriona rushed between him and Royce and shoved at the men to push them apart. 'Neither of you will make any decisions for me. I will make them for myself, and once I have decided, I will let *you* know what they are.'

She sent them both a withering glare and disappeared through the crowd, leaving them staring after her.

Chapter Twenty-Five

'Rolf,' Catriona asked, following her brother down the hall to the armoury, 'what is Royce going to do? Surely he can't kill him for what he said.'

Her younger brother stared straight ahead, moving quickly to keep up with Royce and his men who half dragged and half carried the bloody but still conscious MacGregor down the hallway. 'Aye. He can for what that bastard said about you. Hell, I want to, and I'm not nearly as bloodthirsty as Royce.'

'But what if *I* don't want you to?' she pleaded. The man was a dolt to be sure, but she didn't wish him dead.

'After the things he called you? Why would you *not* wish him dead? He embarrassed you and embarrassed us in our own home. He made a scene. If Royce doesn't respond, then we will be seen as weak, and no Cameron is weak. Not even me.' He stopped in front of the armoury and met her gaze. Anger simmered in his eyes, and the transformation of her easy-going brother into this man was startling. She took a step back.

'Stay here, sister,' he ordered. 'This is no place for you, no matter what you may have seen in your life before.' He walked into the armoury after Royce and sealed the door behind him.

Sickness threatened at the thought of what might happen to Dallan MacGregor, and Catriona rushed towards her chambers. She ran down the hallways as fast as she dared in her fine slippers and long gown. She reached the basin and retched. Just when things in her new life were the best they had ever been, the past yanked her back, reminding her of how small she was in the universe and that good things never lasted. She'd embarrassed her family. Her eldest brother and Ewan had fought with one another over her honour, of all things. And she had been brutally reminded that she was not truly in charge of her own destiny. Even though she was no longer controlled by Thomas, she was still the ward of the men in her life, unless they agreed to grant her the freedoms she longed for, which didn't seem likely.

And any hope she had of speaking with Ewan about a possible future seemed doomed as now he and Royce were at odds. All because Dallan MacGregor had to put her in her place and make a fool of her. Little did he know the shame she had endured in her past. His words were of no consequence to her. If only others understood that. The only words that mattered to her were the words of those whom she loved. Dallan MacGregor would create his own demise; hell, he might already have done just that, as Royce didn't seem a man to grant anyone mercy.

'Well, you certainly made an impression,' Garrick said, helping Ewan up the stairs of Glenhaven.

'Aye. They made an equally memorable impression on me. I believe that might have been my last Grand Highlander Ball at Loch's End.' He nodded to the Stewart soldiers posted outside, and they opened the castle doors for them. Mrs Stevens scurried down the hall and gasped at the sight of him.

'My laird! I thought ye were going to a celebration, not a brawl. What has happened?' She clucked and fussed over him as if he were a chick and she the mother hen.

If he wasn't in so much pain, he might have ordered her to stop. 'Dallan MacGregor happened,' he replied.

'Get some water heated and call for Miss Stewart,' she yelled behind her to the maids.

'Oh, you don't need to—' Ewan began, but it was too late as the maid was already off to fetch his sister.

Garrick cringed. 'You're in for it.'

Ewan cursed, but then smiled. 'Ah, you forget, brother. You will also be in trouble for allowing *me* to get in a brawl.'

Garrick frowned and then dropped Ewan unceremoniously on the closest large chair. 'Deuces. You're right.' He rubbed his forehead.

Brenna came tearing into the room. 'What is this about you being in a—' She stopped short at the sight of them. 'Glory be. Are you hurt, brother?'

Ewan smirked. 'Dallan looks worse.'

Brenna rolled her eyes at him and popped her hands to her hips. 'I choose one ball not to attend alongside you, and this is what happens? And why did you not keep my brother out of trouble, Garrick?' she asked.

'Told you,' Ewan murmured. Garrick frowned at him.

'As you know, your brother manages to find his own trouble whether I am there or not.'

'Are you hurt?' she asked, concern needling her brow. She pointed to Garrick's bloody tunic.

'Nay. I am uninjured. That is your brother's blood that has stained my finest tunic and jacket. He is the one in need of tending to.'

'So, do either of you care to tell me what happened?' she asked, perching on the arm of the chair as she lifted Ewan's chin to look at the wounds on his face.

He pulled his face away. 'Not really.' He wasn't up to another chastisement.

She sent a glare to Garrick who caved under her withering look. 'MacGregor made more than one unseemly remark about Mrs Gordon—I mean, Lady Cameron— and her past. Ewan set him to rights about it. Royce intervened as protector. He then kicked us out for causing a scene at his ball.'

'And Catriona?'

'She is angry at me for trying to defend her honour and protect her,' Ewan said as he touched his swelling lip. 'I have no idea why.'

'You have no idea?' Brenna asked.

'Nay.'

'Garrick, what did he say?'

'He was trying to defend her honour. So was Royce. She lashed out at them both.'

'And?' she asked, tilting her head to the side.

'I said she was my intended and under my care and protection,' Ewan volunteered. 'Royce took issue with that and said she was under *his* care and would make the best decisions for her, not I.'

'So, let me make sure I understand this. You brawled over who was in charge of her in front of a man demeaning her in a room full of people.'

'It sounds worse when you say it like that.' Ewan dabbed his eye with the corner of his torn tunic sleeve.

'Ewan you are a fool,' said Brenna. 'Of course she is angry with you…and Royce. She has lived her whole life with others making decisions for her and controlling her. She wants to make her own decisions and have her own life for once. Can you not understand that?'

He cursed under his breath. He understood that *now*, but it was far too late.

'Deuces. What do I do now?' he asked, rubbing the sore shoulder Royce had almost snapped in two.

'Do you love her?' she asked.

'Aye. I've told you I do.'

'Then you need to think of the grandest gesture you can fathom to make it up to her, and then…do more.'

He let his head flop back against the cushion and sighed. So much for this ball being a chance to win Catriona back. He'd just made his position with her that much worse. He'd tried to control her and treated her like the possession he swore she never was to him.

'Blast. Why didn't you stop me, Garrick?'

'I did, but you tried to punch me in the mouth.'

Ewan cringed. 'Oh. Sorry. I wasn't thinking clearly.'

'Nay,' Brenna answered, crossing her arms against her chest. 'You weren't thinking at all.'

Chapter Twenty-Six

A week had passed since the Grand Highlander Ball, but it felt like a month at Loch's End. Catriona patted her mare's neck. 'Good girl,' she said. The sweet molasses-coloured horse leaned into her touch. 'I know,' she teased. She took a carrot from her pocket and gifted it to the mare, who gobbled it up swiftly.

The ride across the valley and up into the glen was exactly what Catriona had needed. She'd released some energy, and her body felt more relaxed as she stared out towards the rolling hills and glens that would lead up to the edge of the border the Camerons shared with the Stewarts. It would take her less than an hour to make the trek to Glenhaven if she wished, but what good would it do her? Ewan wanted something different than she did. He'd made that plain enough on more than one occasion. He'd also not sent word to her at all after what happened at the ball. He had been silent, as many of the members of the Cameron household had been.

Royce was avoiding her, and Rolf had said little to her after entering the armoury to deal with Dallan Mac-

Gregor, who had been returned alive to his clan, but not without injury. Catriona was just glad he had survived. Susanna was almost her usual self, but Catriona could tell her sister was on edge because of Royce's behaviour. She and Catriona whiled away the hours together as best they could. They spoke of what books they were reading and which ones they hoped to read next. They talked about their dreams and wishes and took exercise out of doors by walking the hillsides when they could. But still Catriona missed Ewan. He was almost always on her mind, and she felt like a bloody fool.

The sound of thundering hooves captured her attention from behind her, and she turned her mount. Her breath caught. It couldn't be. Not here on Cameron lands. She squinted.

It was him.

Laird Ewan Stewart was riding Wee Bit, and they were headed this way, like an imagining from her dreams. 'Steady,' she told her mare as much as herself. 'Steady.'

Ewan slowed as he approached, and Catriona's heart skittered in her chest at the sight of him. Had he ever been so handsome? He wore a pair of dark fitted trews with a crisp white tunic and fine grey coat. His hair was mussed, his face flushed with exertion, and his shoulders were set with a determination she had not seen before. He dismounted and walked over to her.

'How did you get here?' Catriona said.

'Rolf allowed me entry. I am rather sure if Royce had seen me, he would have shot me dead with one of his fine arrows, but it was worth the risk to see you.' He smiled. 'You look lovely.'

'Thank you, my laird.'

'May I speak with you?'

She hesitated.

He placed a hand over her own. 'Please. Just hear me out. If you decide to still hate me, the decision is yours, and I will never bother you again.'

She sighed. 'I do not hate you,' she offered.

'That is a fine start.' He grinned, his dimple and eyes flashing with hope. 'May I?' he asked, offering her assistance to dismount.

She accepted and revelled in the feel of his hands along her waist as she slid off the horse and into his arms. A flash of their embrace in the carriage and all that happened there heated her mind and her skin, which made her shiver.

He rubbed her arm. 'Would you like my coat?' he offered.

'Nay. I am not cold, I am just…uncertain.'

'About me?'

'Among other things.'

He took her hands in his. 'I'm sorry to be one of the things you are uncertain of. I'm sorry for a great deal more. For pushing you away in the carriage because I feared you would leave me for the Camerons and never return. For acting like a royal arse by making you feel like a possession at the Grand Highlander Ball. That was never my intention. And I am most sorry for not being the man you deserve. The man I want to be for you.'

She blinked back at him. Such an apology she had never imagined. She was struck dumb.

He let go of her hands and retrieved a fine fabric pouch from his pocket. 'This is for you.'

She took it from him, pulled on the string to open it, and poured a guinea attached to a chain onto her palm. 'What's this?' she asked.

He picked it up from her palm and placed it around her neck. 'I realised there was nothing I could give you that you couldn't get for yourself now that you are a Cameron, so I made you something to show you that you will always have your freedom if you choose me as your husband. That I will encourage you and support you in all your endeavours, even the clarsach.' He smiled.

She laughed and her eyes welled. 'But what of love? I cannot be in a marriage where love is not allowed. That is a rule I cannot follow, for I love you. Dearly.'

Ewan closed the space between them and ran a thumb over her cheek before holding her face close to his own. 'There is one more thing I am certain of. I will love you more and more with each passing day until I am but dust on this earth, Catriona.'

'So you will cast aside your rule?'

'I will cast aside many things for you. My pride, my fear, my pain. All of it. We can build a life together based upon truth, trust, and openness.'

'And love?' she added.

'And love. We will build our life together on that promise as well,' he answered. 'Will you be my wife, Catriona? Do you dare choose me?'

'Aye,' she answered. 'And I will choose you each day over and over and over again.'

He seized her mouth and kissed her.

The rush of knowing that she would kiss him, be held by him, and be loved by him for the rest of her days filled her heart with a hope she had never felt before.

'So, when shall we marry, my laird?'

'Is tomorrow too soon?'

'Perhaps. But any day after that shall be fine.'

He laughed against her lips. 'Then, any day after tomorrow it is.'

Epilogue

Three months later

Ewan watched at a distance as the meadow overlooking the valley below was alive with music, laughter, and dancing. The Cameron and Stewart clans were celebrating his marriage to Catriona earlier that morn. Sun beamed across the grasses, and the sky was as clear a blue as a bluebird's wing. He could scarce believe she was now his wife and that he felt such an unabashed hope for his own future and the future of the clan as he looked along his lands and his home of Glenhaven.

'You have done what we all believed impossible,' his sister Moira said, snuggling up to Ewan and laying her head on his shoulder. He wrapped his arm around her and hugged her. He had missed her far more than he would ever admit.

'Do you mean by finally choosing a bride?'

'Nay,' she said, poking him in the arm. 'I mean how you have kept us all together as a family and a clan, just as Mother and Father would have wanted. It is a miracle, and you are responsible for it.'

His heart tightened in his chest. Had *he* done that? He looked around the field and saw Brenna and Garrick, now wedded and expecting their own bairn, smiling and playing with his nephews and nieces while Catriona stood arm in arm with her sister Susanna. Even Royce smiled as he drank from his tankard and chatted with Rolf, the rift between him and Ewan mended over their common love and adoration for Catriona.

Royce had also finally confessed the reason for his initial coldness to Catriona: shame. He was the one who had encouraged her to chase him into the water the day she disappeared, and he felt responsible for her being pulled out to sea. Of course, Catriona assured him that feeling responsible for what happened to her was foolish and unwarranted, but Ewan understood Royce's guilt, and such an understanding had become a tether between them.

Peace between the Cameron and Stewart clans was restored and even improved, and the Stewart clan elders no longer worried about the future with such a renewed alliance forged. The clan was also making changes to protect its future with Ewan at the helm and Catriona by his side. He had also learned to trust love again and to love as he never had before, and so had his siblings. What more could a laird and brother ask for?

Catriona waved to them from afar.

'I believe your wife has need of you,' Moira whispered. 'Just as poor Rory has need of me. I believe one of the twins just stripped off their plaid.'

Ewan laughed. 'Go then and see if you can gather that tartan before Rufus steals it, and I will see to my wife.'

'Aye,' she answered, ruffling his hair before she left him.

Ewan grimaced and attempted to smooth his hair back down before heading to his wife, who had started to walk towards him as well. When they reached each other, he kissed her and pulled her to his side.

'Do you know what I am most grateful for other than you and our family?' Ewan asked.

'Wee Bit?'

'Other than our animals.'

'Glenhaven?' she answered.

'That too. But I am most grateful that Brenna needed a new hat. Otherwise, I would have never seen you that day in the market.' He smiled. 'Look at our families. They are happy and celebrating in a way I would never have thought possible. And all to honour you, me, us, and our clans.'

'Aye. And I have found a family lost to me for decades and added a new one as well,' she said.

'My mother used to say to not worry because nothing that is meant for you will get past you in your life, even though it may take its time in getting to you.'

'I like that,' Catriona added. 'So, I need not worry about my first riding victory against you. Since it is meant for me, it cannot get past me. I will just bide my time until it is the right moment for it to happen.'

'No rush, Lady Stewart. We have the rest of our lives to get the timing just right.'

* * * * *